R

CONTRACTED:
A WIFE FOR THE
BEDROOM

CONTRACTED: A WIFE FOR THE BEDROOM

BY

CAROL MARINELLI

MILLS & BOON®
Pure reading pleasure

First published in Great Britain 2007
Large Print edition 2007
Harlequin Mills & Boon Limited,
Eton House, 18-24 Paradise Road,
Richmond, Surrey TW9 1SR

© The SAL Marinelli Trust Fund 2007

ISBN: 978 0 263 19498 2

Set in Times Roman 17 on 19¼ pt.
16-1107-48852

Printed and bound in Great Britain
by Antony Rowe Ltd, Chippenham, Wiltshire

CHAPTER ONE

'SMILE!'

Using the rear-view mirror to paint on her lipstick, Lily could almost hear her childhood ballet teacher's affected tones calling out for her to look happy and relaxed as she performed some excruciatingly painful manoeuvre.

And tonight's group session *was* going to be excruciating—happy and positive were the absolute last things she felt this evening. Even an hour spent in front of the mirror, sweeping her blonde hair back in a smart French roll, carefully applying her make-up and dressing in her most snappy navy suit hadn't enabled Lily to muster the confident air that usually surrounded her. No amount of power dressing was going to save her tonight! The only thing she had to show for weeks spent wrestling with banks, real-estate agents and mortgage brokers was a pounding headache and the appalling re-alisation that, this time, she couldn't protect her mother.

Now she had to go in there, into the community centre, and imbue confidence, try to convince these people that they could be anything they wanted to be, could attain any goal, if only they truly set their minds to it.

She felt like a charlatan.

Dabbing a touch of concealer on a tiny pimple on her chin, Lily wished that life was so easy—that she could wave her magic wand and make problems disappear. Only problems didn't disappear, Lily thought darkly, watching as, despite fifty dollars a dab, her pimple shone through.

Slipping off her silver thongs, Lily rummaged on the passenger floor for a pair of high-heeled sandals, slipping her feet in and doing up the thready laces, wishing she were actually taking them off—wishing that this day, this night was well and truly over.

Not that they weren't divine.

A mere inch of suede had somehow been crafted into the softest, most divine of foot couture—accentuating her duskily painted toe-nails—the spiky heels magically elongating her ankles, somehow adding that extra oomph Lily so badly needed tonight.

'Come on, shoes,' Lily whispered, feeling a touch like Dorothy clicking her heels. 'Do your stuff.'

Thick, heavy dots of rain hitting her wind-screen dragged her out of her introspection and Lily knew that if she didn't want being drenched to add to her woes, then hiding in her car wasn't an option. The end of a long hot sultry spell that had hit Melbourne was, according to the forecast, about to be broken by a storm. Dashing across the car park, Lily just made it into the centre before the rain took hold, and as she stepped inside and saw her clients waiting for her, some standing alone and nervous-looking, as if they might flee at any moment, some mingling in groups, drinking the questionable coffee all turned to greet her as she entered. Lily's smile wasn't as false as she'd anticipated—she felt genuinely glad to see the familiar and new faces of people who were looking to her to help them change their lives.

'Good evening, everyone.' Lily glanced up at the clock, glad to see that she was ahead of schedule. 'Carry on chatting among yourselves for a while. I'm a little early so we'll give everyone a chance to get here before we start.'

Pulling paperwork out of her briefcase, Lily did a brief head count, ticking off the names on her list and putting out self-help brochures for the group to take away if they wished. She smiled warmly as a very new, very nervous, participant entered the room. Blushing and painfully shy, the newcomer blinked as she looked around the room, wringing her hands nervously as she stood there, and Lily's heart went out to the stranger. She admired the huge step this

woman was taking by coming tonight and immediately crossed the room to welcome her.

'My name's Lily,' she said warmly, offering
her hand. 'Welcome to New Beginnings.'

'Amanda,' came the nervous reply. 'I didn't
know if I needed an appointment.'

'Not here,' Lily said. 'I just need you to fill
in a form and then you can grab a coffee and
start getting to know a few people—we really
are a very friendly lot!'

Helping Amanda through the form took a little
while longer than normal. Amanda, as Lily found
out, had recently lost a huge amount of weight,
followed by her marriage, followed by the little
confidence she'd possessed, but Lily could tell
that behind the shy façade was a very strong
woman and one Lily couldn't wait to see emerge.

'Right, that's all the paperwork done.' Taking
the clipboard from Amanda, Lily was about to
suggest that she get a drink when her attention
was caught by the door opening—well, not so
much the door opening, more the man that was
coming through it!

Her first thought was that he must be lost.

He didn't look lost—anything other than that but men like the one appearing in the doorway did not belong at a self-help group meeting at the local community centre.

No, men like this one belonged in the middle of a glossy celebrity magazine or strutting his stuff down the catwalk, or—Lily gulped, blushing at the thought—they belonged in the giddy realms of a very private erotic dream.

She'd seen him somewhere before, Lily was sure of it, though simultaneously she doubted it because, if that were the case, *surely* she'd remember *exactly* the moment, for he was stunning.

Stunning!

Tall, long-limbed and lean with rakish good looks, his very dark brown hair, which was clearly superbly cut because as he dragged a hand through it it spiked into a perfect messy shape—his ice-blue eyes worked the room. Lean but certainly not skinny, Lily decided as he peeled off his jacket and shook the rain from it; beneath his white cotton shirt you could just tell his body was toned and muscular. His presence was so commanding it literally stopped the room, every head turning as he stood there for a moment, holding out his jacket as if he expected someone to collect it for him.

Someone *did* collect it for him!

Jinty, the housewife who till recently had washed down her morning cereal with a glass of vodka and orange, was first in the queue, taking his expensive jacket and hanging it on a peg as everyone else in the room, Lily included, sucked in their stomachs like a reflex action, staring in open-mouthed admiration at this Adonis who quite simply didn't belong in suburbia.

'Can I help you?' Lily attempted to greet him as she would any other newcomer to the centre, by walking across to him and trying to put them at ease—not that this man appeared remotely uncomfortable. Quite literally he oozed confidence. It was Lily who was having trouble remembering how her legs worked, Lily feeling like a child in her mother's high heels as she teetered across the room and offered her hand to this stunning stranger. 'I'm Lily Harper.'

'Then I'm in the right place,' he drawled in a *very* well-schooled voice, 'I'm here to join the New Beginnings Group.'

'Oh!' Lily blinked, and then corrected herself, trying to remember to treat him like a mortal, trying and failing not to judge, to attempt to fathom what could possibly have bought him there. 'Well, welcome!' She was still holding his hand, pumping it up and down as if she expected to find water! 'I just need you to fill in a form.'

'Sure.'

Sure, Lily repeated to herself, peeling her fingers from his hot grasp, trying not to appear flustered as she made her way to the table and handed him a clipboard with the necessary form attached. Only she was flustered—very!

He smelt divine, like walking past the aftershave counter at an exclusive department store, Lily thought as she absorbed the heavy scent he emanated, trying not to notice the piercing blue of his eyes or the chiselled planes of his impossibly handsome face. 'Do you need a pen?'

'Please.' He stared at the rather grubby, very well-chewed pen that was being offered and then without a word declined, heading over to his jacket and producing one he, no doubt, deemed more suitable, before coming back to the table where Lily was now thankfully seated. The chatter in the room resumed again, but rather more subdued now, everyone's ears on elastic, trying to hear his answers as Lily walked him through the form.

'There's no need to put your surname,' Lily commented, 'or your address, though we do ask for your postcode.'

'Fine.' He was sitting loosely cross-legged beside her, resting the clipboard on one long slender thigh, leaving it for Lily to guess where he was up to on the form. 'I like your sandals, by the way.' Somehow he managed to address the form *and* run an experienced eye along the length of her calves right down to her toes, which Lily felt curl on cue.

'Thank you.' Lily coughed, every exposed inch of flesh blushing as she tried to concentrate on the blessed form. 'We ask for your salary range—if it falls in one of top three categories—'

'It does,' he interrupted.

'Then in that case…' Lily gave another small cough— more than anything she *hated* discussing money. 'We ask if you'd consider paying towards the cost of the session—depending what category you're in…'

'The top one.' He squinted at the piece of paper. 'Easily.'

'Then we ask you to contribute fifty dollars, but you can always pay next time if you don't have it with you tonight, and if for some reason finding the money is a problem, please, don't let it stop you from coming to the sessions—it really is a voluntary contribution.'

'It's no problem.' He pulled out a very sleek wallet and peeled off a note.

'I'll write you a receipt.'

'There's really no need.' He resumed filling in the form as Lily ignored him and started to fill in a receipt. 'Tell me something.' Thick beautiful eyebrows almost met as he frowned over at her. 'Why, if someone is earning in the top category, would you offer for them not to pay? It doesn't make good business sense.'

'This isn't a business.' Lily smiled. 'New Beginnings is a community-funded programme—it's available to everyone, rich or poor. Anyway, for all I know…' She stopped talking then, but still he stared.

'Go on.'

'Well, you might have just come from the casino and lost everything, your business might have collapsed. There are many reasons people find themselves at this sort of group—it certainly isn't for me to judge your circumstances solely on the box you tick.'

'Glad to hear it.' He frowned down at the last bit of the form. 'What exactly do you want to know here?'

'Well, as the question suggests, we're trying to find out what brought you to New Beginnings.'

'It was suggested to me.' He shrugged.

'What do you hope to get out of it, then?' Lily smiled patiently. 'Most people are here for a reason, they're hoping to change a part of their life or want some guidance with goal setting, to help them move onto a better one—it just helps me if I know what you're hoping to achieve…' Her voice trailed off as he started writing again, and she couldn't be sure but there was a slight smirk on his mouth as, tongue clearly in cheek, he finished off the form and handed it back.

'Thank you,' Lily said, deliberately not peeking at what he had written, though she was aching to! 'Here's your receipt. Now, we'll be moving through to the meeting room in five minutes or so. If you'd like to grab a coffee before we start, you're very welcome.' She pointed over to the urn, but he shook his head.

'Just an iced water, thanks.'

He was joking, surely! But from the expression on his face he was clearly expecting her to stand up and fetch it for him, clearly *very* used to having people run around after him.

Well, not here!

It was Lily shaking her head now, managing not to smirk as she answered his rather derisive request.

'There's a water fountain at the entrance.' She gave a very sweet smile. 'Please, help yourself to a polystyrene cup!'

Hunter.

She stared at his extravagant handwriting, trying to glean a little more from his rather sparse summing-up on the form. He was 32 years old, he came from an exclusive city suburb and earned in excess of the top box. None of that came as a surprise—everything about him screamed of excess, from the exquisite tailoring of his suit that skimmed his sculpted body to the flash of a heavy gold watch on his wrist and the bunch of notes he'd peeled the fifty-dollar one from. Even those icy blue eyes hinted at excess, slightly bloodshot with purple smudges beneath them, and the tiny squint as he had filled in the form had Lily wondering if he was recovering from one too many nights on the town.

Hunter Myles—even though he hadn't put his surname down, suddenly it came to her—that rather dangerous face placed now. He was a brilliant financier—not that Lily read the business pages much, she only skimmed through them if they'd moved her horoscope—but Hunter Myles had become somewhat the darling of housewives everywhere, writing the odd quirky little piece in magazines and offering share tips that over and over had proven golden. And now he appeared occasionally on breakfast television and regularly in *all* the social pages—a loose cannon in the staid world of finance, his party lifestyle legendary in the last year or so since... Lily frowned in concentration. There had been some tragedy, some accident, something that had sent him skidding off the rails in such spectacular style... Oh, what was it, now? And what, Lily wondered, was he hoping to achieve from New Beginnings? Staring at the form, Lily raised a neatly plucked eyebrow.

Inner peace!

Oh, his tongue had been firmly in cheek as he'd written it. Lily had seen the smirk on his face, known that he was being glib—but there was one tiny chink in his impressive armor that she'd noticed, manicured but undoubtedly bitten nails had drummed on the table as he'd spoken and there had been a restless energy that had belied his confident stance. He might have been joking when he'd written it but, like everyone else, maybe inner peace *was* what Hunter was seeking.

'Welcome, everyone.' Lily beamed around the meeting room. 'Tonight we have two new members—Amanda and Hunter. Now, the point of a group session is to share and encourage, so let's take our time to introduce ourselves.'

Lily listened as the group worked clockwise, listening as Richie told of his hopes for a deeper, more meaningful relationship after the demise of his marriage, as Jinty spoke about her battle with the bottle and her hope for a more sober, fulfilling existence and onwards until they came to Amanda.

'Well.' Blushing furiously, she looked down at her knees. 'My marriage ended recently. I thought that if I lost weight it would help to save it, but it just made things worse.'

'How much have you lost? If you don't mind my asking,' Lily checked.

'Over fifty kilograms. I know I've still got a way to go—but I feel as if I'd like to join the world again.'

'That's a huge achievement.' Lily smiled as the group clapped their encouragement, all except Hunter, that was. Apparently bored rigid by the proceedings, he was practically falling asleep in his chair and Lily resisted the urge to give him a sharp kick on the shin before turning her attention back to Amanda. 'When you say you're ready to join the world again, in what way?' Lily asked, nodding encouragement.

'I'm trying to get up the courage to join a gym,' Amanda said shyly. 'I know I should just do it, it's just the thought of walking in there, having everyone looking at me.'

Lily made a note on the pad in her lap as

Amanda carried on talking. 'I'd like to look for a job as well and who knows? Maybe one day…'

'Go on,' Lily said gently, as Amanda's voice trailed off. 'You're among friends here.'

'I'd like to think about having a relationship—you know, get out there…'

Everyone in the group was nodding encouragement, offering congratulations on her huge achievement, everyone that was except Hunter. He was leaning back on the sofa, yawning unashamedly, not remotely moved by Amanda's story and clearly thoroughly bored with the whole proceedings. Lily felt a flash of anger— what the hell was he doing there if he thought he was so superior? Well, she was going to find out—if this Hunter thought his story was so much more interesting than everyone else's, it was time to hear it!

'Hunter.' Lily snapped him to brief attention. 'Perhaps you'd like to introduce yourself to the group, share with us all a little of what bought you here tonight.'

Perhaps not! The silence was interminable as

he stared back at her and she felt impossibly hot and uncomfortable under his scrutiny and annoyed, too, that he could be so at ease with the pause in the proceeding *he* had created. 'You've written that you're hoping to achieve inner peace.' She flashed a brittle smile. 'That doesn't tell us anything, Hunter—everyone in this room is hoping to achieve that.'

'The teacher, too?' There was more than slight insolence to his question and Lily determinedly didn't redden, that bubble of anger in her starting to swell as somehow he managed to mock the proceedings that were taking place.

'Yes, Hunter, even the teacher.' Almost imperceptibly her eyes narrowed but her smile stayed intact—she was determined not to judge until she'd heard his story but years of working with people had given her an incredibly sensitive radar and it was bleeping loudly now. For reasons she couldn't fathom, this man was here under false pretences, wasn't in the slightest bit interested in joining in with the group. He was quite prepared to just sit there and let the whole group share their innermost thoughts and give absolutely nothing of himself. She knew all about shyness, knew all about people who needed some time and space before they could even begin to open up, but Hunter exhibited none of the usual nerves. 'Most people come to a group like this for one of two reasons— either a major life event has forced them to re- appraise their goals or they've realised after some soul-searching that something is missing in their lives and they would like to make more of themselves.'

'Really.'

'Are you happy in your work, Hunter?'

'I don't really have time to stop and think about it.'

'Do you make sure that you have some time when you're *not* thinking about work?'

'I never think about work when I'm in bed.' He gave her a very small but very suggestive smile and despite herself Lily felt the beginning of a blush spread over her cheeks. This man was incorrigible, but he redeemed himself slightly when finally he addressed the group. Not that he needed to redeem himself to them—they were eating out of his hand. 'Well, as you probably all know, my main expertise is in futures, though I do have other interests.'

'You're a medium!' Jinty breathed, gaping in admiration.

'Hunter's referring to the stock market,' Lily corrected, smothering a smile as Jinty inadvertently brought him down a peg or two. 'Am I right?'

He gave a gracious nod.

'What about your personal relationships?'

'What about them?'

Lily sucked her breath in in irritation, he was playing them all along and quite simply she wouldn't allow it. She looked around at the eager, kind faces of her clients and knew she had to protect them. Putting down her clipboard on the table in front of her, Lily wasn't smiling any more, her green eyes *very* serious as she faced him, her mouth opening to speak, to tell him what she'd never told a client before—that their time at New Beginnings was about to end—now!

He'd pushed her too far—as easily as he read financial spread sheets, Hunter could read women, and he knew, just knew that this was one unhappy lady. And she really was a lady, from the tip of her blonde hair down to her prettily painted toenails, her trim figure soft and voluptuous in *all* the right places. She had naturally what so many manufactured—effortless beauty and grace. He flashed her a winning smile, but it failed to move her, those gorgeous almond-shaped green eyes narrowing, tense lips opening, and Hunter realised that for once flirting wasn't going to save him. He was almost tempted to add another flip comment, curious, actually, to see how she handled herself, but, remembering the reason he was there, Hunter halted himself.

Emma.

His stomach tightened—the guilt that was ever present these days upping an uncomfortable notch as he recalled Emma's pale, anxious face when she'd asked him to check out New Beginnings for her. And for that reason alone Hunter deigned to concede.

A touch.

'I've actually just broken up with my girl-friend.' Hunter's remorseful words beat Lily's sharp ones and, giving a beautifully timed, regretful shrug, he played the sympathy card perfectly, cast his net to the engrossed audience and dragged them all willingly in. 'We were about to get engaged—she'd even chosen the ring.'

'I'm sorry to hear that.' Surprised by his admission, Lily took a second to regroup—she'd been so sure another smart reply had been about to come, had been *positive* he'd reveal absolutely nothing about himself. She was also certain, well as certain as one could be from reading the glossies that Hunter wasn't in a serious relationship—but pushing her doubts aside, remaining professional, Lily dealt with the facts as Hunter saw fit to give them. 'How long did the relationship last?'

She watched as he squinted, tried and failed not to notice just how gorgeous he looked as he did so, dark hair flopping over his forehead as he counted on his fingers. 'Two,' Hunter started. 'No, maybe three…' His voice faded out as he did the maths and magnanimously Lily tried to help him.

'Two years might not sound like a long time to some here.' Lily smiled over at Richie, whose ten-year marriage had recently ended. 'However, just because Hunter's relationship is marked in years rather than decades—'

'Not years,' Hunter broke in, 'months. We were together for two months.'

An interminable pause followed—Lily casting her eyes around her group and trying to fathom how to incorporate Hunter into it, trying to give this impossible man a chance. 'The end of a new relationship can be devastating,' Lily attempted. 'That first flush of passion, the sheer heady emotion of those first few weeks can evoke intense feelings of grief when it ends. Isn't that right?'

'I guess,' Hunter admitted, to Lily's relief. After all, Abigail *had* cried her eyes out.

'Overwhelming feelings of loss,' Lily offered.

'Well.' He nodded. 'Abigail did seem *very* upset.'

'Who ended this relationship, Hunter?' Lily asked, confused by his response.

'Me,' he answered, as if the answer should be obvious and giving her a slightly startled look, which Lily chose to ignore.

'And you chose to end it because…'

He frowned before answering, actually looked as if he was thinking about the answer, and Lily found she was holding her breath.

'She bored me,' Hunter answered finally, as Lily's head jerked up. 'I mean, she was great to look at, fabulous in bed but, at the end of the day I guess that she just bored me. They always do in the end.'

'In what way?' Lily asked, remembering her training, though sorely tempted to slap his cheek. 'Is it the woman herself that bores you or the thought of monogamy?'

'I've never really given it much thought,' Hunter shrugged, clearly bored with the subject, but Lily smiled and nodded.

'Well, the end of a relationship is always a good time for introspection—a time to look at needs and wants that may have been stifled, to work out what we really want, not just from a partner but from ourselves. What would your ideal relationship be, Hunter?'

'As I said.' He sounded just a touch irritated now. 'I haven't really given it much thought.'

'Well now's your chance!'

He stared at her for the longest time and Lily decided there and then that his name was very apt—he looked like a hunter, someone who chose his prey carefully then pounced, because those blue eyes on her were hypnotising in their effect. He was so utterly a predator that Lily felt the hackles on her back rise in defence as he eyed her thoughtfully.

'I want to wake up with someone in the morning and actually want to hear what she has to say. Someone who embraces her feminine side but isn't intimidated by my masculinity. I guess what I really want…'

'Go on,' Lily croaked, suffused suddenly with images that were surely inappropriate—his masculinity, his good looks, his raw sensuality were not only intimidating but incredibly thought-provoking, and trying to stay objective and focused as Hunter discussed his needs and wants was almost an impossible task.

'An equal,' Hunter finished, blinking at his own admission. He was getting quite good at this, he thought. 'An equal, though not an identical half.' He elaborated a touch.

'That's very perceptive,' Lily said, running a tongue over dry lips and dragging her eyes away from his to address the group at large. 'Hunter has made a very valid point. Equality in a relationship is vital for its success—both partners valuing the other's contribution to it and embracing the other's individuality. All too often, however, I hear people saying that they want a relationship as if it's the solution to all their problems. The relationship that you need to nurture is the one with yourself. I believe first and foremost in self-love—'

'I don't have any problem with that,' Hunter interrupted. 'But as a last resort, of course, I prefer the real thing!'

Lily swung her head around, and she wasn't the only one. The whole group gaped at Hunter, who didn't look remotely abashed as he happily bought up the most delicate of delicate subjects.

'When I refer to self-love…' Lily cleared her throat, wishing that she'd bought her own poly-styrene cup of water into the session '…I meant self-respect, actually liking yourself, knowing your own opinions, being at ease with your own company. Only when you've achieved that can you truly step into a relationship as an equal.'

'Oh, that!' Hunter dismissed.

By the time the rest of the group had intro-duced themselves, Hunter had dozed off, his head drooping forward slightly, those knowing eyes mercifully closed. Lily decided that rather than waking him, to just let him sleep off whatever excess he was suffering from. But as the meeting continued, though she tried to give her all to her clients, tried to listen intently as Jinty spoke at length of her hope for staying sober and finding a new partner, and Richie spoke shyly about his first date in a decade, Lily could sense her own distraction, her eyes constantly drawn to him. Even while asleep he unsettled her; even while quiet he interrupted her thought process at every turn.

What *was* he doing there?

CHAPTER TWO

'HUNTER!'

The third and final call had absolutely no effect. All the plastic chairs had noisily been put away and yet *nothing* had woken him up.

For a second Lily actually considered walking away, throwing his jacket over him and leaving him for the cleaners to find in the morning. But integrity took over, and finally, almost scared to touch him, she tentatively reached out and shook his shoulder, feeling the solid mass of flesh beneath her fingers.

'Hunter, the session ended fifteen minutes ago.'

'Did it?' Lazily he stretched and yawned, testing every inch of her patience as he languorously stood up and peered around the room, locating his jacket and rather unsteadily putting it on.

'Is there any chance of a coffee?'

'The urns been put away.' Lily frowned at him. Gorgeous he may be, but those stunning eyes were clearly having trouble focusing. 'Are you OK to drive?' Lily checked; her natural assertion and training enabling her to deal confidently with this potentially difficult situation. 'If you've been drinking, it might be wise to call a taxi.'

'I don't drink,' Hunter answered.

'At all?'

'I tried it once and didn't like it.'

'You seem…' Lily gave a small nervous swallow. If he hadn't been drinking then he must have taken something—he was swaggering slightly as he walked.

'If you have taken something then you really ought to think about—'

'I'm not on drugs!' He caught sight of her worried frown and actually smiled. 'Unless you count an overdose of caffeine. I'm fine, just a bit jet-lagged.'

'Jet-lagged?'

'I flew in from New York this morning, or was it yesterday?' he squinted down at his watch. 'It's still yesterday there.'

'Have you slept since?' Lily asked, worried now about him driving and feeling just a touch guilty for her earlier assumptions—he had every right to look a little the worse for wear.

'Just then.' He gestured to the room they'd left. 'Don't worry, I'll be fine. Tell me something,' he asked suddenly. 'Do you really believe that if you set your mind to something you can make it happen?'

'To a point,' Lily answered carefully, wondering where this was leading and realising that even though apparently asleep he'd taken in more of her session than she'd realised.

'That anyone can better themselves.'

'Of course.' Lily answered immediately. 'Unless, of course, you're already perfect.'

Her stab at sarcasm just drew a lazy smile from him. 'Oh, I'm far from perfect, and I certainly don't wake up in the morning and kiss the mirror and tell myself I'm beautiful and worth it.'

He was teasing her and again Lily realised that he'd actually been listening all along.

'I don't actually kiss the mirror but, yes,' Lily admitted, 'I do encourage self-affirmation.'

'Till true love comes along and then he can do it for you?' He raised his eyebrows, mocking her with his words, but Lily stared right back and shook her head.

'You have no idea what I believe, Hunter. I encourage self-love because I actually believe that the only relationship you can truly rely on is the one you have with yourself. A lot of people don't want to hear it so I don't say it. I hopefully get them to a point where they're happy and confident in life and then the rest is up to them.' She knew he didn't quite get what she was saying, those knowing eyes narrowing slightly, a vertical crease in that perfect brow, and she told him her truth—revealed to him what she actually thought. 'The truth is, I don't actually believe in love.'

'Really?'

'Really.' Lily nodded. 'I believe in lust. I believe in romance. I believe in mutual respect. But I truly don't believe there's one love for everyone, one love that can last a lifetime.'

'Amanda will be very disappointed,' Hunter said.

'Amanda's not going to hear it from me,' Lily retorted equally quickly, assuming the conversation was over and turning to head for the door. But Hunter lingered, the derisive note gone from his voice now.

'What about someone with, say, disabilities?' Hunter frowned. 'I mean, suppose for instance that someone had been told they could never walk again. Are you saying that if they really set their mind to it…?'

'I'm not offering miracles, Hunter,' Lily answered softly, ending the verbal sparring, sensing for the first time genuine confusion behind his words, wondering if perhaps she was about to find out what really had bought Hunter there tonight. 'If someone who's been told they'll never walk again is focusing solely on proving the doctors wrong, they're missing out on a lot of other opportunities. Maybe it's better to expend that energy on different goals…'

'Give in, you mean?'

'I'd prefer to call it acceptance.'

'That's how you make your living I guess.' Hunter barbed response didn't faze Lily this time—she knew his anger wasn't aimed at her.

'Just who are we talking about here, Hunter?'

'No one.' He flashed a brittle smile. 'It's just a hypothetical question. Right…' For Hunter it was clearly conversation over. He held out several thousand dollars' worth of the finest, most beautifully spun wool. 'Do you want to borrow my jacket?'

'Your jacket?'

'It's pouring outside,' Hunter needlessly pointed out as they were having to raise there voices now to be heard above the driving rain that was bouncing off the roof.

'I'll be fine,' Lily declined, smiling to herself at the thought of using such a beautiful garment as a temporary umbrella and filled with strange regret that once he stepped out into the night she'd never see him again, that whatever her group offered it wasn't something he needed. Lily was filled with curiosity, too, as to why on earth he had come. He intrigued her. He was so utterly, utterly confident, so breathtakingly opinionated, and yet, on occasion—she looked at the proffered jacket—when Hunter wanted to be, he was disarmingly nice.

'Take it,' he offered again, his hand completely steady as he held it out to her, a curious half-smile on his face, but as she raised her hand to accept it suddenly everything changed. In that instant Lily knew, just *knew* that it was more than a jacket that Hunter was offering, knew from the way he was looking at her that the seemingly simple gesture had dangerous conno-tations and that stepping out into the night with him would be like stepping out with the devil himself. Brutally aware they were alone now, she felt like Snow White with the dwarfs all out at work, a tempting apple being thrust unexpectedly in her face. Telling herself she was crazy, that she was completely overreacting, she struggled to centre herself, to push away the ridiculous thoughts that were flooding her mind.

'Lily?' Softly he questioned her indecision but she couldn't answer. His chest was at her eye level, the rate of his breathing matching her own, awareness, attraction swirling around her like a heavy fog, seeping into her clothes, her flesh, her mind.

She could smell *them*—not just the mingling scent of their colognes, but the perilous undertones beneath, the thick lusty yet indefinable smell of arousal, and it made her feel dizzy, confused and more than a little claustrophobic.

'No!' She didn't even attempt politeness, instead snapping the word out, his unvoiced question meriting no well-mannered response.

'Your choice.' Hunter shrugged.

And it was surely the right one.

Watching as he stepped out into the night, Lily dragged a shaking hand up to her hair, staring around the room and blinking at the normality of it. Surely somehow the windows should be broken, tables and chairs should upended, that there should be some evidence of the seismic shift that that had just taken place.

What the hell had happened there? Lily tried to fathom, her breathing still coming out short and uneven, her heart still thumping loudly in her chest, every sense on high alert as if she'd just chased out an intruder. He'd offered her a jacket, for heaven's sake, yet she felt as if they'd kissed, *more* than kissed… She felt as if he'd seen inside her, *felt* inside her.

Flicking off the lights and stepping out into the pelting rain, Lily was actually grateful for the sting of the wind and rain, the cool change incredibly welcome after such a scorching encounter. Locking up behind her, Lily made a mad dash across the car park, her suit clinging to her drenched body, her French roll uncoiling as she unlocked the car door and, shivering, jumped inside, dreaming of a bubble bath up to her neck to soothe away the tension of the day…

It wasn't over yet!

The day that had started so badly with a phone call from her mortgage broker went from seriously bad to downright disastrous as her engine spluttered noisily, emanating a huge grating sound that seemed to get louder with each and every frantic turn of her key. A mechanic Lily wasn't—truth be known she didn't even know where the catch was to lift the bonnet—but even to Lily's untrained ears the sound was perilous enough to tell her that the only journey her car was taking tonight was on the back of the vehicle rescue truck.

The passenger door opening momentarily panicked her—she'd thought the car park was empty and Lily wasn't sure if it was the force of the rain and wind that caused her to catch her breath or the gorgeous but somewhat intimidating sight of Hunter climbing in beside her.

'Most people knock on the window,' Lily reprimanded.

'I'm not like most people. 'Problem?' he added, stating the obvious for the second time since he'd climbed in the car beside her, because he really wasn't like most people.

He disturbed her.

Spun her into a state of heightened nervousness, though not for her safety. An excellent judge of character, there was nothing in his personality that made Lily feel that her safety was compromised, her nervousness, her state of hyper-vigilance when he was around entirely due to the dangerous feelings he evoked.

'Do you know anything about cars?'

'I like silver ones.' He gave a dry smile as Lily gritted her teeth. 'I suppose I could do the macho thing and ask you to pop the bonnet and stand there staring for a few thoughtful moments—are you wearing stockings?'

'What?' Lily did a double-take. 'What on earth has that got to do with anything?'

'I saw it on a film, I think…' He frowned for a moment. 'Or did I read it? Anyway, it's entirely irrelevant because I'd have no idea what to do even if you were wearing them—I haven't a clue about cars.'

'Well, thanks for your *help*.' Lily gave a tight smile.

'I haven't given you any help yet,' he pointed out. 'Why don't I give you a lift home? You can sort out the car in the morning.'

'I'll be fine,' Lily said, reaching for her mobile phone. 'I'll ring the rescue service.'

'They could be a while. Cars will be breaking down and skidding into each other all over the place tonight.'

'Then it's just as well I'm a patient person.' Despite her curt refusal of his offer, Hunter made no move to go. In fact, he didn't even shift himself as Lily was forced to lean over him and delve into her rather messy glove box and retrieve her car manual. He sat drumming his fingers on his leg as Lily rang the number and after an impossibly lengthy time of being placed on hold she gave in and punched in the number for a taxi.

'No luck?' Hunter asked needlessly, having listened to her rather exasperated one-sided conversation.

'I've been placed in the queue.'

Which meant she was there for the duration. Staring out into the dark night, the rain lashing at her windscreen and no prospect of escape for the next couple of hours at best, Lily decided that if he offered again she'd let him take her home. After all, she'd been worried about him driving—this way she could make sure that he was OK and give him a quick coffee before he headed off to his house.

Happy with her decision, she waited expectantly, a frown forming on her face as Hunter opened the passenger door.

'Well, good luck,' he said. 'I hope you're not waiting too long.'

Damn! Lily cursed in her mind as he swung his legs out, yet still she was sure he was testing her, sure that he would offer again.

But clearly he wasn't into games. Even as the thought formed she was privy to the rather gorgeous sight of him, lean and long-legged, briskly walking across to his car, and Lily knew if she didn't do something she'd be stuck her for ages, knew that he'd left it to her to make the next move.

A man like Hunter didn't need to offer his services twice.

Even as she threw her keys and phone in her bag and opened the car door, even as she locked her vehicle and dashed across to his sleek silver car, Lily knew the decision she'd made, though on the surface it appeared rational, was perhaps the most dangerous, illogical thing she'd done in her life. Thumbing a lift on the freeway would possibly be more sensible—better the devil you didn't know perhaps. Yet she wanted to do this and was curiously elated that fate had intervened and her brief dalliance with this unforgettable man wasn't yet over.

His headlights came on, illuminating her in the darkness, and for a second Lily froze, blinking into them, drenched and exposed. She could envision the glint of the triumphant smile that was surely gracing that surly, beautiful mouth. This was a man who liked to be in control.

Unlike Hunter, who'd so boldly climbed into her vehicle, Lily went to tap on his window, but already he'd opened it, staring up as if he'd been expecting her, his hair damp and flopping over his forehead, music wafting out of the car's stereo, his hands loosely holding the leather-covered steering-wheel. Never had a car looked more inviting or more dangerous.

'That lift you offered.' Her teeth were chattering and it had nothing to do with the temperature. Despite the pelting rain, the night was still warm, the shiver running through her having everything to do with his eyes lazily drifting over her before finally deigning to meet hers. 'If you still don't mind…' Still he stared, not saying anything, forcing her to ask him outright. 'I'd love a lift home.'

'Sure.' With the tiniest motion of his head he gestured to the passenger side and Lily dashed around, her heart in her mouth as she opened the door and climbed in, feeling the soft leather on her damp legs, the warmth of his car stifling, the music too loud, his erotic scent stronger in the stuffy, luxurious confines, every sense bombarded with confusing messages as she momentarily entered the world of this intriguing man.

CHAPTER THREE

HUNTER had turned down the music as she'd given her address and Lily felt she had to fill the rather awkward silence that ensued.

'I'm sorry if this is out of your way.'

'It isn't.'

'It really is very kind of you…' Her voice trailed off and Hunter did nothing to fill the painful silence, made absolutely no attempt at small talk. Truth be known, where she lived wasn't particularly out of his way, she knew from the form he had filled in the suburb where he lived, but had she not been in the car no doubt he'd have taken the freeway and driven the rather more direct route to the city. Instead, he moved the car skilfully along the wet roads and took the longer but infinitely prettier beach-road route that would take them to her bayside apartment.

The view was divine. Staring out the window, Lily stared into the inky waters of the bay. Rolling clouds obliterated the moon, just angry spears of lightning illuminating the bay, the moored boats bobbing in the storm, the waves pounding the piers as his car silently gobbled up the distance. But the electric tension in the air outside was nothing compared to the energy in the car, the atmosphere so thick she had to drag the air into her lungs, the silence deafening as a million questions buzzed unvoiced between them. Never had her apartment complex looked so welcoming—normality soothing as the end to this strange encounter was finally in sight and Lily gestured for him to pull up. 'This is where I live.'

'Where do you park?'

And it sounded like a normal question, only it wasn't. He should have indicated and pulled into the kerbside, perhaps waited for her to offer him a drink, but instead he was gliding the car into the driveway as his eyes searched for her private parking space. It felt incredibly invasive as he glided into it and pulled the hand-brake and turned off the lights and ignition, just assuming that he was going to be asked in.

'I could really murder that coffee.' He flashed a beautiful smile as she gave a tense nod, her whole body rigid as he followed her through the concrete maze of the car park and into the entrance of the apartment complex. She fizzed with awareness, even the most normal of tasks, like walking, made infinitely more difficult, her feet slipping inside her saturated sandals. She was excruciatingly aware of her damp clothes clinging to her body as he casually strolled along beside her. As she turned the key and pushed open her door, Lily blinked in wonder at the untidy familiarity of her own apartment, as if somehow it should have prepared itself, should somehow have known who was coming home with her tonight.

Her dinner plate and mug was still on the coffee-table, a top and bra she had pulled out of her closet and promptly discarded when getting ready lay strewn over the back of her sofa, and a pile of magazines and newspapers lay lazily next to a mountain of bank papers.

'Excuse the mess.' She marched through to the kitchen, hoping he would follow so she could dash out in a couple of moments and do a frantic clean-up, but Hunter wasn't going anywhere, except to the sofa. He sat down and stretched his long legs out, crossing them at the ankles. Her lacy pink bra hovered, apparently unnoticed a few inches from his cheekbone, as he picked up a magazine and idly thumbed through it.

'Nice apartment.' He glanced up briefly.

'It is when it's tidy,' Lily answered.

'I like it like this.' He went to turn back to the magazine then changed his mind. 'I usually get the more sanitised version of a woman's life.'

'Sorry?'.

'Immaculately tidy, fresh flowers in the vase, a few highbrow books on the coffee-table...' Lily gave a shocked giggle of recognition as he described how her apartment would have looked had she known he was coming. 'I prefer the real you.' He held her eyes for an indecent amount of time and Lily could feel herself colouring under his scrutiny, his blatant flirting unnerving her. She wanted to go and get changed, put something warm and safe on, yet she couldn't imagine heading to her bedroom while he was in her home. Thankfully he averted his eyes and turned back to the magazine he was reading as he dismissed her. 'Three sugars, please,' Hunter said, not even looking up as he relegated her to waitress. 'And lots of cream.'

'You'll be lucky if I've got any milk,' Lily muttered, heading off to the kitchen, flicking on the kettle and pulling out only one mug, choosing instead to pour herself a glass of wine from a bottle in the fridge. After the day she'd had—was still having—surely she deserved it.

A quick coffee and he was out of here, Lily decided, watching her shaking hands attempting to spoon coffee into a mug. Perfectly behaved he may have been since he'd set foot in her apartment, sitting quietly on her couch, reading, pleasant about the mess, even adding a 'please' when he'd requested his sickly sweet beverage, but she felt as if there were a wild animal in her lounge, a sleek black panther—infinitely beautiful yet dangerously unbridled, an untamed predator—just a few feet away.

Do not feed the animals. Staring into her rather bleak pantry, Lily managed a wry smile—she couldn't if she wanted to.

Taking a deep, calming breath, Lily headed back to the lounge, but any attempt at composure vanished as she saw Hunter sitting on the sofa, calmly reading her financial papers and barely looking up as he offered his unwelcome opinion.

'You can't afford it.'

'What the hell are you doing?' Shaking with rage, Lily just managed to put the drinks down with out spilling them before ripping the papers out of his hand. 'You don't read people's private documents!'

'Why not?' Hunter shrugged, completely unperturbed by her fury. 'There's no quicker way to get to know someone. Tell me, Lily, why on earth would you want to take on such a massive mortgage?'

'That's none of your business.'

'On the contrary—money *is* my business.'

'Oh, that's right,' Lily flared, 'because you work on the stock market, because you're featured in some magazines and appeared on television, you think you're entitled to poke your nose into everyone's private affairs?'

'I don't work *on* the stock market—I *work* the stock market,' Hunter corrected calmly, an utter contrast to Lily's trembling rage. 'More often than not to my advantage. People pay a lot of money for my opinion and I'm giving it to you free—I'd listen, if I were you.'

'I don't have to listen,' Lily bristled. 'I already know that I can't afford it—I already know that the banks are not going to lend me the money and that the house…' Suddenly it all caught up with her, the tension of the past few weeks, the frustration of feeling so helpless all culminating into this moment, all her fears magnified as this impossible man forced her to confront what she already knew. Tears stung her eyes as she resumed talking, her words more to herself than Hunter as she admitted the unpalatable truth. 'It's going to have to be sold.'

'Sold?' Hunter frowned, staring again at the papers. 'I thought you were looking to buy… Oh, I see.' He flicked over a couple of pages. 'This is your parents' house.'

She was too exhausted to be angry as he shamelessly delved further into her documents, the anxiety that had propelled her in recent weeks utterly depleted now. Sitting on the sofa beside him, Lily took a sip of wine and leant back, closing her eyes as Hunter questioned her further.

'My mother's,' Lily corrected him her voice a monotone. 'My father died two years ago.'

'So it's solely in your mother's name?' Without even a murmur of acknowledgment to her loss, Hunter dealt with the facts. 'Why do you want to buy it?'

'Because my mother can't afford it—she's defaulted on her loan.' Lily let out a long tense breath. 'She was planning to turn it into a bed and breakfast in the hope of keeping it. She's up in Queensland now, talking to her sister about coming in with her, but things have just started to snowball. I just found out that there's going to be a mortgagee's auction in two weeks and unless she comes up with the money...'

'But if she can't afford it, surely she's better off downsizing,' Hunter responded, his voice utterly void of emotion, just as the bank manager's and the umpteen lenders she had dealt with over the past few weeks had been. For Lily it was the last straw.

'Says who?' Lily's voice was shrill. 'She's lived in that house for thirty years, all of her memories are there—her life. Why should she lose it?'

'Because she hasn't got the money to keep it,' Hunter said blandly, utterly unmoved by her emotive outburst. 'Why does she owe so much if she's been there so long?' God, he was direct—no skirting around the edges, no gently feeling his way into a conversation. He was business personified. 'Didn't your father have insurance?'

'They took out a new mortgage to pay for my father's treatment and to spend his last year travelling.'

'That was rather selfish!' Hunter rolled his eyes. 'Didn't he realise the mess he'd be leaving for your mother?' Lily's mouth gaped open, stunned at what she was hearing, reeling that he would *say* such a thing, but Hunter stared coolly back. 'Don't tell me you haven't thought the same.'

'Maybe...' Lily blinked rapidly, feeling sick at her confession to a stranger. 'Perhaps a bit, but you don't know the circumstances, and you have no right—'

'Fine.' Shuffling the papers into a neat pile, he placed them down on the table and picked up his coffee, dropping the difficult subject, leaving Lily to freefall with all the emotion he'd just triggered as he calmly drank his coffee in a couple of gulps then stood up. Even though she hadn't wanted him to stay, suddenly she didn't want him to leave, curiously deflated as this wild animal took one sniff of the air and seemingly meekly walked away.

'Thanks so much for the lift.' Lily stood up and walked him to the door.

'No problem. Thanks for the coffee.'

'You'll be OK to drive?'

'Why? Are you worried about me?'

'You're a client…' Lily attempted, but he shook his head.

'No.' Very deliberately he excused himself and Lily felt the hairs on the back of her neck stand up as he took away that moral dilemma and plunged her into a rather more personal one. 'I was never there for me—I was checking the place out for someone else. So, you see, I'm not your client, which means you have absolutely no need to worry about me—unless, of course…' boldly he stared '…you want to.'

'But you said…'

'I'm not into group therapy.' Even the most bland of words were laced with innuendo when

Hunter said them, even the most subtle flick of his eyes had her head spinning. 'I prefer things to be one on one. I really was just there to make sure that things were aboveboard for…' He hesitated for a fraction. 'A friend.'

'And were they?'

'Very.' He nodded. 'And the coffee was most welcome, but now it's time to go, I can tell that I've annoyed you.'

'A bit,' Lily admitted, 'but that's my problem, not yours.'

'Do you do it all the time?' Hunter asked, still staring unashamedly, but it was his mouth rather than his eyes that held Lily's attention now, thick sensual lips that barely moved as he spoke, but his words were all silkily measured. 'I mean, everything someone says—do you analyse it? How can my obnoxiousness be your problem?'

A sliver of a smile shivered on her own lips, countered by a nervous pink tongue bobbing out, and it was as if they were writing their own rules for flirting, the manual that said eye contact was so important tossed aside as they both concentrated on a more subtle erogenous zone. For Lily the effect was devastating, her mouth rendered almost immobile, words stammered out in a breathless voice as her lips ached for his. 'It-t i-isn't—my reactions are m-my own.'

'Well, I'm glad I can evoke a reaction.' The irony of his statement wasn't lost on Lily. Never in her life had a person evoked such a reaction, her mind, her body spinning with awareness, dizzy from a host of new sensations. 'And I am sorry if I offended. I have this terrible superiority complex, you see. I know I'm always right.'

She was actually smiling now, terribly reluctantly but she was definitely smiling, and in that unguarded second he pounced, well, not pounced, but for the first time he touched her, his fingers picking up a strand of damp blonde hair and tucking it behind her ear. Even though she stood stock still his touch felt like a dam was bursting somewhere inside, rivers of awareness, arousal coursing through her as his free hand took the glass she was clutching and placed it carefully on the hall table.

'Tonight's been…' He paused while he chose his words. 'Unexpectedly pleasant.'

'I'm glad I didn't bore you.'

'Far from it.' He frowned quizzically at her. 'Can I ask you something?'

'Why bother checking?' Lily gave a rueful smile, but it covered a nervous swallow. She somehow sensed what was coming next, almost knew what he was going to ask her. 'Why would a pretty little thing like you give up on the pot of gold?'

'I don't understand.'

'Oh, but I think you do!' He was pinning her with his eyes as he voiced a question most would never have dared. 'How did someone as young and as beautiful as you get so cynical?'

'Cynical.' Lily smiled and frowned at the same time—cynical was the *last* word that she'd use to describe herself. She adored her life, her family, her friends, was happy, motivated and truly believed that the world and the opportunities it offered were there for the taking.

'Yep, cynical,' Hunter insisted. 'All this talk

about not believing in love—maybe you shouldn't knock it till you try it.'

'I tried it once and didn't like it.' She threw his own words back at him but despite her best attempts Lily's dismissive voice couldn't disguise the pain that was there.

'What happened?'

'I don't want to talk about it.'

'For someone who makes a living getting people to open up, you're incredibly reluctant to share.'

'There's not much to tell.'

'Try me.'

Her eyes jerked to his, saw the challenge that was there and met it head on. 'OK, then. I was engaged for two years—we were actually going to bring forward the wedding in the hope my father would be able to come.'

'But?' Hunter asked because clearly there was one.

'My father took a sudden turn for the worse—and two days before he died I found Mark, my wonderful fiancé, in bed with my supposed best friend. There—is that enough information for you?'

He didn't respond to her sarcasm and again he offered no sympathy, didn't even acknowledge her pain, just fired another direct question. 'So you ended it?'

'No.' She watched his eyes narrow at her response. 'I was too busy dealing with my mother, the hospital. There was just so much going on…' Her voice wobbled a touch and Hunter jumped in.

'You didn't even confront him?'

'Nope…' Her eyes glittered with unshed tears. 'I just put it in the too-hard basket. The last thing Mum needed was more upset—she was really close to Mark, and for all the world Mark was the perfect fiancé when my father died. You should have seen him take over, calling relatives, arranging the funeral, even holding my hand through the service. I can still hear everyone telling me how lucky I was to have him—in fact, if I hadn't seen it with my own two eyes, I'd never have believed he could be unfaithful. I'd probably be married to him now if I hadn't found out—still be living in a fool's paradise.'

'Where is he now?'

'With Janey—my one-time best friend. Apparently, as Mark likes to tell it, I was a bit depressed after my father died and froze him out—they still insist that nothing happened for months after we broke up.'

'You're better off without them.' Hunter shrugged, not remotely moved by her story. 'But one swallow doesn't make a summer.'

'Sorry?'

'So, your ex was a bastard—hardly enough to judge an entire species by.'

'It was enough at the time,' Lily countered, but two spots of colour were burning on her cheeks, his scrutiny unnerving as he refused to accept her sorry tale.

'Come on, Lily, you're a sensible girl—relationships end for far less—you probably were a right old misery to be with at the time. Now, I'm not saying he was right to do what he did, but I'm sure you can see where the relationship started to go wrong.'

'Are you always this sensitive?'

'Not always.' Hunter responded to her sarcasm with a brand of his own. 'But given we've only just met, I didn't want to be too harsh.' He stopped teasing then, his eyes assessing her for the longest moment, his voice serious when finally it came. 'What else happened to you, Lily?'

'Nothing!' She answered him too quickly, her voice a touch too shrill, and if she'd been strapped to a lie detector it would have blown a fuse at her pathetic attempt at denial. 'Isn't that enough to be going on with?'

He stared at her through narrowed eyes and Lily dragged hers away, his scrutiny unnerving, as if somehow he could see deep inside her. But just when she thought he'd push harder, just when she was on the verge of maybe even telling, thankfully, regretfully even, he pulled away. 'For now,' Hunter said, pulling his car keys out of his pocket, and turned to go. 'Thanks again for the coffee.' He smothered a yawn as he walked out of the door and no doubt out of her life. Lily was gripped with something akin to sadness, biting down on her lip she fought the impulse to call him back, not realising that Hunter was battling with demons of his own.

He didn't want to go home.

Didn't want to ring Emma and tell her about his evening—didn't want a night rattling around his apartment on his own. But more than that, he didn't actually want to leave Lily.

And it wasn't just because she was gorgeous—beautiful women were ten a penny in his word. If it was just sex or company he wanted, he had plenty of willing participants—it was *this* gorgeous woman that enthralled him.

Drenched, miserable and exhausted, she'd still given him her time—and unlike so many others she expected nothing from him.

Nothing!

Jangling his key on his index finger, heading for his car and a music-fuelled ride home, something stilled him.

Something he couldn't define made him pause and turn around.

'I really am fine to drive...' Very slowly, very deliberately he turned to face her. 'I'd just rather not.'

Her eyes jerked to his and the lust blazing in them was so blatant there was no question of mixed messages, his meaning utterly, utterly clear. As Lily stared back, transfixed, she begged for reason to descend, for her usually ordered mind to focus, to give an appropriate response to his terribly inappropriate proposal.

She wanted to say yes!

One hand was leaning on the wall behind her as his other smoothed another imaginary lock from her forehead, tracing again the path he had blazed so easily before, infinitely kissable lips literally a breath away, the taste of him an imagined delicacy on her tongue, and lust battled with reason. Surely she'd regret this. To contemplate sleeping with this man was something every woman in his path surely did, but to actually fathom it, to *know* that for tonight at least all this could be hers, was a conundrum Lily had never in her life envisaged. He was as out of place in her bedroom as he had been at the community centre, a divine prototype that didn't belong in the parameters of her existence. Yet here he was, adoring her with his eyes, lifting the silver lid and tempting her with laden, flambéd plates of passion—the ultimate, most elicit dessert menu thrust in front of her to break her diet. She toyed mentally with the delicacies on offer, knew that a flavor of nectar would surely sour her tastebuds for ever, that to taste him now could only render any future offerings lacking.

But she wanted this.

Wanted to taste him, to feel him, wanted that moment on her lips to spend a lifetime in her memory…

The brush of his mouth on hers almost made her faint, her flesh swelling with ripeness as he graced her with his presence, a tiny shocked gasp as instead of a kiss, first he licked her, his tongue tracing the Cupid's bow of her lips, then bit her lower lip, and if it had been anyone else she'd have recoiled, but not with Hunter, it was the single most erotic thing she had ever experienced in her life—and it wasn't transitory, tasting her, circling her lips, till he *had* to stop, till he had to end this delicious torment with a kiss…only he didn't. Instead, he gently bit into her lower lip, sucking her till she was swollen, till her body was writhing with want, yet his hand was still leaning lazily on the wall behind her as he urged her body closer with sheer magnetism.

Then he kissed her.

She'd *never* been kissed like this before. He tasted divine, his lips moving slowly against hers, almost lazily, but his indolent lips served a purpose—such a contrast to the hard skilful motion of his tongue, creating a frenzy in her body, his tongue cold against hers, until it was Lily pressing her lips harder on his, Lily wanting the full weight of the passion he had allowed her to glimpse.

And he reciprocated, in the tiniest but most erotic of ways, his hand moving to the small of her back. Long-fingered, warm-palmed, the weight of his hand didn't guide her forward, just radiated a heat that moved her closer to him. Pressed against him, she was lost. Lost in a the sensation of his sensual body, the lean, toned hardness of him, the heady smell of him, the luxurious feel of his hair beneath her fingers. All she wanted was for this kiss to last for ever, to feel as she did at this moment, while knowing it couldn't, their bodies just too aroused to linger in this ecstatic moment for long. And when Hunter broke the spell, moved his mouth away a fraction, Lily couldn't believe what she was contemplating but couldn't fathom saying no either.

'We c-can't…' She stammered the words out, breathless, stunned. Still reeling from his kiss, she attempted reason.

'Why not?'

'Because…' Her mind flailed for a suitable response but how pathetic *any* excuse sounded when her body was screaming otherwise. 'I'm not into one-night stands.'

'Who said anything about one night? I like you, Lily—I think I could get to really like you.'

'It's not that easy…' Her breath was coming out in small hard gasps. 'I don't know a thing about you.'

'There's plenty of time for that.' His hand was still on the small of her back, more firmly now, welding her to him, letting her feel his hardness, glimpse what could be hers—for tonight at least and tomorrow at best. Because, despite what he was saying, Lily knew she could never hold him, that for him the flare of attraction would be extinguished the second the real world invaded or his needs were met.

But?

Didn't she always say to go with one's instincts, to listen to that inner voice? And right now hers was screaming! Her instincts were all pointing in one direction only—this beautiful, beautiful man who was here and now, who was making her feel more of a woman than she had ever felt in her life, who was offering her a delectable sample of what she could never really own. And it was truly easier to go with the flow than reject him on principle. Up close and personal with Hunter was the most intoxicating experience in her life to date and one she wanted to savour for as long as the moment allowed.

'Lily.' There was almost a pleading note in his deep sensual voice as his lips nuzzled into her neck. Her eyes closed in submission as he pressed his lips harder to her flickering pulse. 'I don't want to sleep alone…'

He was peeling her jacket off—no invitation required, pulling her top over her head in one easy movement, expert fingers unhinging her bra. She felt the shift as her breasts fell plumply into his waiting hands, felt the swell of arousal as his fingers worked her nipples, his tongue hot now as he licked her areola in painful, ever-decreasing circles, teasing the swollen centre with a glimpse of his velvet caress but never quite taking it fully in till she begged.

Till she took his hair and guided him, till she placed his mouth where it was needed now, and even though she'd never been one for one-night stands, the 'casual' in sex an enigma to her, she'd never been in the hands of a master before, never felt the rush of blood to her most private places, beaten only by the heavy pad of his finger. His mouth worked on, suckling her till surely she would come in his mouth.

Without even asking direction, he kissed her into the bedroom, mouth, hands everywhere as he slid her along the hallway wall, discarding her clothes *en route.* He switched on the light, for which she was pathetically grateful, because if there was ever a body to see naked it was his.

He undressed *himself. He* dealt with every practicality, stood over her as she lay shivering with want on the bed as he disrobed. And it was the most erotic thing she had ever seen—the slow teasing opening of a decadent parcel, more blissful with each revelation, her nails digging into her palms as he unbuttoned his shirt. No torturous waxing for Hunter, the smattering of black hair fanning his broad chest, circling his dark nipples, making her stomach curl inside.

Wide-eyed, drunk on arousal, she watched with almost fascinated terror as he slid down the zipper on his suit pants. Biting down hard on her bottom lip, she shivered out a greedy moan at the stunning delicacy on offer. Slender-hipped, with a toned flat stomach, his flesh was generous in *only* the right place, his black pubic hair silken and unusually straight, as if warning Lily of the rarity of the treasure she was viewing. And as he knelt on the bed beside her, it was impossible not to reach out, impossible not to touch him.

'Careful,' Hunter warned, but she was way beyond that, caution long since blown to the wind, feeling the soft velvet skin beneath her fingers, the potent hardness alive in her hands as his mouth drank from hers, drowning as he pushed her down further, as with practised ease he slid on a condom and parted her knees with his thighs.

'Don't move.' It was an impossible order. He was stabbing at her entrance, filling her slowly, and she wanted to move with him, to drag him in deeper, for him to fill her, but Hunter was insistent. 'You're not to move until I say you can.'

Eyes wide open, he stared down at her as he teased her with the first inches of his generous member, till she was weeping out loud, his hands a vice-like grip on her hips as she fought the urge to move with him. Yet when she started to, when her body couldn't play to his imposed tune, he upped the stakes and pinned her down with his full weight, till all she could do was taste him, taste the salt of his chest as he slid over her and within her, giving her a little more of himself with each measured thrust, till finally he released her, not with his body but with one shuddering word.

'Now!'

She coiled around him, arched into him as her body spasmed into a heated frenzy, her fingers digging into his taut buttocks as he filled her completely, and each deep contraction of her orgasm should have been the last, but it went on and on for ever—even when he'd spent himself inside her tiny beats of pleasure protested the ending.

'Oh, Lily…' He groaned the words out, buried his exquisite head in her neck and dragged in her scent, holding her so fiercely that the gamut of emotion she witnessed through him captured her with yet another twist, because if making love to Hunter had been the most heady, intense, extreme encounter in her life, then the infinite tenderness he expressed afterwards was an enigma. She'd almost braced herself for the cruel mental slap of him dressing and leaving, but instead that supreme body was spooning into hers as he held her close and drifted to sleep. Feeling his breathing, the silk of his skin against hers, the strength of his arm protectively holding her, Lily realised something.

She hadn't wanted to sleep alone either.

CHAPTER FOUR

SHE could feel his eyes on her as Lily's mind awoke before her body, knew he was watching her as she slept. His gaze felt like a caress. She felt as if she were being drawn by a skilful artist, the drape of the sheet over her body, his eyes bringing out the most feminine, beautiful aspects of her, just as his body had done last night.

Opening her eyes, all Lily could do was smile, the guilt that she would normally have felt after such a reckless night utterly absent. Propped up on one elbow, he was blatantly staring at her, only it didn't feel uncomfortable. His face was even more exquisite than she remembered, those cool blue eyes not mocking or superior, just caressing her as she gradually came to, stretching like a cat in the warm, tousled bed, feeling the blissful warmth of his hand on her stomach.

'Morning.' His hand was idly stroking her stomach through the sheet, actually not so idly, Lily realized. The soft, circular motion was having a definite effect. 'What are your plans for today?'

'Hmm?' Lily was only half listening, her eyes closed again, concentrating instead on the wonderful sensations he was drawing out of her awakening body, trying not to think about climbing out of the warm bed that bore the sharp lingering scent of the passion they had shared last night. Wanting to hold onto the fantasy of them just a little while longer. Hunter's caress was infinitely more pleasurable than having to deal with a broken down car and her financial worries.

'Because,' Hunter continued, clearly wide awake and raring to go, 'we could go and look at your mother's house.'

'Why?' Lily frowned.

'Well, don't you have to water the plants or let out the cat or something?'

'She lives more than an hour's drive away in the Red Hill area.' Lily laughed. 'The cat would be crossing its legs!'

'Why don't we go anyway?' Hunter insisted. 'I haven't had a day off for ages. I'll ring Abigail and tell her to arrange it.'

'Abigail?' Lily checked. 'Your ex—she works for you?'

'She's my PA,' Hunter nodded. 'Why?'

'I though you said you two were finished.'

'We are,' Hunter answered. 'But just because our…' He paused for a second, 'For want of a word *relationship* is over, there's no reason I should lose a perfectly good PA. She was upset at the time, but Abigail's fine with it now.'

'You're sure?' Lily frowned.

'Absolutely. She knows the two of us couldn't have worked out and at the end of the day she loves her job too much to quit over something so petty.'

Petty.

His choice of word confirmed every idea Lily had formed about him in their few hours together. Relationships were a mere trinket to Hunter—a small, pleasurable diversion and absolutely nothing to lose a moment's sleep over. But nothing Hunter said would convince Lily that it was so easy for Abigail. Sure, she'd never met the woman, but there was no way one could go on seeing this man every day and not want him.

He was addictive.

From the first second that she'd laid eyes on him, nothing else had mattered except getting more of him, not just sexually but emotionally and mentally as well. Like a fabulous book that kept one up all night, turning the pages, like a nibble of the most delectable chocolate that had you peeling back the shiny foil for just a little bit more, he consumed all thought processes, created need where there had been none. Seeing him every day and not having intimate access to him would be torture—like an alcoholic working in a bar—the fix constantly at arm's length but utterly out of reach. And after just a single night in Hunter's arms

Lily knew it could never be that easy. That the time they had shared was going to be a memory that would linger for ever.

'I guess it would be prudent to see it before I buy it.' His words snapped her out of her daydream, but Hunter hadn't yet finished with his ludicrous suggestions. 'I think we should get married.' Just like that, he said it, sort of drawled it as he if were commenting on the weather, or suggesting that they go out for breakfast. 'What I need is a wife.'

'So do I!' Lily grinned. 'Preferably one who loves ironing and cleaning and one who know how I like my coffee.'

'No, I've been *really* thinking about it,' Hunter pushed.

'So have I,' Lily said. 'One sugar—it's your turn to make it.'

'Not till you answer my question.'

'I wasn't aware you asked one.'

'I mean it, Lily. I've been lying here since the crack of dawn, going over and over it, and marriage is the perfect solution.'

'To what?'

'Your money problems.'

'My money problems aren't your concern.'

'But I could buy your mother's house for you.'

'Why on earth would you want to do that?'

'Stability.'

Lily hadn't actually expected an answer to her question, but if she'd tried to fathom his response, that would have been way off the list, but even before she could respond he elaborated.

'Some of my major investors are starting to get testy about my lifestyle.'

'Hardly surprising!' Lily smiled, but it faded as she saw that Hunter was completely serious.

'It's not just my investors. I'm trying to get some big sponsors on board for a charity do I'm organising and it's been suggested that I tone things down a touch, portray a more stable image.'

'And marrying a girl you've known for less than twelve hours will achieve that?'

'My PR people will take care of that.'

'Hunter.' She smiled up at him. 'Last night was fantastic.'

'I know.'

'Completely out of character for me,' Lily continued, ignoring his sheer lack of modesty, 'yet utterly fabulous nonetheless. But, as strange as it might seem to you, all this talk of marriage is rather ruining my one wild night of reckless passion.'

'It *is* the wrong way round,' Hunter conceded. 'I mean, normally I wake up the morning after and she's the one asking about our future…'

'She?' Lily checked, trying and failing not to wince at his answer.

'Whoever.' He was leaning over her, one hand still on her stomach as the other fiddled with her clock radio, filling the room with traffic reports and news bulletins as Hunter bombarded her with his own headline news.

'It would make my sister happy.'

Lily blinked at him in disbelief. 'Since when did a man marry to make his sister happy? Hunter, I thought you'd be the last person to give two hoots what people think, let alone marry for that reason. What you're proposing doesn't make a shred of sense.'

'It does to me. Emma needs to get on with her own life—she's using me as an excuse not to take up a brilliant offer.' He paused for a second, clearly debating whether to elaborate. To tell her the truth. She could feel him mentally weighing her up, and whatever test she was unwittingly taking, she must have passed, because after an age Hunter elaborated. 'She's a violinist—an extremely talented one. She's got a solo part coming up in a few weeks and if that goes well, she's tentatively been offered this huge part in a recital in London. But she's talking about not taking it. She keeps coming up with random excuses— "We're all that's left of the family." "If I travel, too, then we'll never see each other."' Hunter gave an incredulous laugh. 'She's even got it into her head that she needs to be in Melbourne to keep an eye on me. I tell you, she'd come up with any excuse to put off going.'

'You've really lost me now.' Lily shook her head to clear it, but Hunter didn't give her a chance, just bombarded her all over again.

'Emma's disabled,' he explained. 'She suffered spinal injuries in the same accident that killed my parents last year.'

'How awful!' He stated it in such a matter-of-fact voice that it served to exacerbate Lily's shocked response 'Oh, God, I think I remember reading about it. Hunter, I'm so sorry!'

'Hardly your fault.'

'But even so...' Lily said, reeling at the horror of it all and confused by the blandness of his voice. 'Hunter, it must have been a nightmare for you.'

'Well, it wasn't exactly a barrel of laughs at the time, but it was far worse for Emma.'

'Your sister?' Lily checked. 'Is that who you were talking about last night?'

'Yep.' Hunter gave a grim nod. 'She's having a lot of trouble coming to terms with her injuries, but this offer's huge—she really needs to act on it.'

'Maybe she's not ready,' Lily ventured, but Hunter scorned her attempt.

'She's ready—she's brilliant!' He gave a low laugh. 'She's just got too much time on her hands. She's actually starting to believe what the press says about me has a semblance of truth.'

'And does it?' Lily found she was holding her breath as his face darkened, but even as he opened his mouth to deliver a flip response he changed midway, his expression serious rather than angry, those blue eyes holding hers as he spelt out the terms of his offer.

'I'll buy the house for you and any gifts I give you naturally you can keep—believe me, I'll be more than generous. But no one must know it was anything other than a whirlwind affair that in the end went wrong.'

'Went wrong?'

'I'm only asking for twelve months, Lily. Twelve months would give Emma a chance to get her life back without worrying about me, give my investors and sponsors a chance to calm down—then we both walk away with no regrets. I'll buy you that house—'

'You're actually serious?' Lily gaped at him, open mouthed. For most of the conversation she'd thought he'd been joking. Not about his sister, of course—there was nothing to joke about there— but it was starting to dawn on her that Hunter's marriage proposal hadn't entirely been a whim. Even if he'd only thought about it for five minutes, he *had* actually thought about it.

'Oh, I'm completely serious,' Hunter said in a voice that told her he was.

'Why me?' Lily asked.

'Why not you?' Hunter countered. 'You're beautiful, funny, very sexy… I can think of a lot worse ways to spend the next twelve months.'

'But you could have anyone. Why not Abigail or—?'

'Because they'd go and do something stupid like fall in love and think it was for ever,' Hunter interrupted. 'Whereas you and I know that there's no such thing.'

'Right.' Pulling back the sheet, he climbed out

of bed, leaving Lily reeling as, naked as the day he was born but infinitely more desirable, he picked up his mobile, punched in a number and promptly cancelled his appointments that day. 'Think about it,' he mouthed, before turning his back on her and giving an incredibly compli-cated list of orders for the unfortunate Abigail.

And strangest of all—she did. As she stepped out of bed and in somewhat of a daze headed to the shower, as she massaged shampoo into her hair and hastily shaved her legs in prepara-tion for their impromptu outing, it wasn't the amazing night they'd shared that filled her mind. Instead, it was the amazing future Hunter was offering that consumed her.

Not the house. Though that would be good.

Not the car.

Not the money.

But him.

Twelve, exclusive months with this enthrall-ing, breathtaking man.

How could she *not* think about it?

CHAPTER FIVE

'NICE?'

Hunter glanced over at her and Lily gave a nod. She could literally feel the tension of the past few days seeping out of her as they left behind the city.

Choosing what to wear for a day in the country with someone so divine was no mean feat. She'd promptly ruled out the shorts and sandals she'd usually put on, just in case Hunter decided to visit some smart restaurant on the way. After umpteen agonised combinations, finally she'd settled on a khaki skirt that zipped up at the front, a white cotton blouse that knotted at the waist and some cream espa-drilles—and then had spent an inordinate amount of time applying make-up that hopefully didn't look like she was wearing any as Hunter had drained the entire contents of her hot-water system and then had had the nerve to ask her to fetch an overnight case that he kept in his car!

And now here she was snuggled in the soft leather seat of his car as it ate up the miles, sneaking surreptitious looks at Hunter. Out of his suit he still cut a very impressive dash— unshaven, dressed in black jeans and a black T-shirt. Those piercing eyes hidden behind dark sunglasses, he looked sultry and dangerous and utterly untamable. His toned body brimmed with a restless sexual energy that had Lily fluttering with awareness. Absolutely the type, Lily thought with a smile, that mothers warned their daughters about.

'I needed this,' Hunter said. 'I haven't had a day off in as long as I can remember. Not a *real* day off,' he elaborated. 'You know, without my computer or phone.'

They'd left their mobile phones behind. A small detail but it had seemed so deliciously reckless at the time as they'd planned their temporary escape from the world.

'I feel as if I'm playing hookey from school!' Lily smiled, stretching out her legs in front of her and wallowing in the gorgeous feeling of elation and freedom.

'Did you do that?' Hunter asked a hint of surprise in his voice at her admission. 'You look like such a good girl!'

'I only did it once.' Lily visited the memory and then laughed. 'Actually, this feels *nothing* like playing hookey from school. You're right, it was completely out of character for me. Some friends and I went to the movies, but I spent the entire time panicking we'd be seen or that the school would have noticed and rung my parents, so that it wasn't enjoyable at all. I think I still dread my mother finding out! What about you?'

'I did it all the time.' Hunter shrugged.

'Didn't you worry about getting caught?'

'I was *always* getting caught. I had endless arguments with my parents and the teachers…'

'Did they suspend you?'

'Hell, no. I was their top student. They didn't want to blot their academic record by bumping me off to another school—they knew I'd come in the top one per cent of the state when I took my finals. So I had them by the balls and I knew it!' He actually laughed, a deep, low laugh that was as rare as it was infectious, and Lily found herself grinning as he carried on talking. 'I told them that when they had something interesting to teach me or something I didn't already know I'd turn up, which I did, but I certainly didn't need someone guiding me through a textbook.'

'So it's always been easy for you?'

'Believe me,' Hunter said darkly, and something in his tone caused a shiver to run through her, the easygoing conversation ending abruptly as the tension in the car rocketed, 'it wasn't easy.' He frowned at the road ahead and Lily gave a small swallow as they drove in silence.

'Sorry, I just—'

'Assumed,' Hunter finished for her, the harsh edge to his voice breaking the closeness they'd created, relegating her to the rest of a world he clearly thought didn't understand him. 'It's a common enough assumption—people make it all the time.' Lily turned, taking in his tense features, realising then how painful it must have just been for him to talk about his parents after such a huge loss.

'You must miss them.'

'Who?'

'Your parents!' *Of course!* Lily thought, but didn't add it.

'Why?' He glanced over at her shocked expression. 'You know the saying—you can't choose your family.'

'I guess…'

His face was grim—his hand so tight on the steering-wheel his knuckles were white. Lily's mind raced for something to say, to fill this impossible abyss. Clearly he didn't want to talk about it, but in a surprising move it was Hunter who filled the strained silence, Hunter who actually revealed just a little bit more of himself.

'My father had MS—multiple sclerosis,' he explained. 'From the day he was diagnosed he just gave up. He actually wasn't that bad, well, not compared to some, but instead of fighting it, instead of dealing with it, he immersed himself in his own misery and tried to take everyone down with him. He made my mother's life a living hell. I can still hear his stick banging on the bedroom floor when he wanted something—still see my mother running up the stairs to reach him before he banged again. I don't know why she didn't leave him.'

'Maybe she—'

'Loved him,' Hunter broke in. 'We've already established there's no such thing. I asked her why she didn't just go, why she didn't just leave him to wallow in his own misery.'

'You actually asked her?' Lily reeled at his boldness.

'Yep. She pointed out that we had a beautiful home, her children went to the best schools, that even though he was sick he was still earning good money—he invested in real estate,' Hunter added. 'She also pointed out that without her help he wouldn't be able to work, that all the luxuries would disappear— she said it was her duty to stay.' He let out a low mirthless laugh. 'She never understood that I'd have lived in a bloody tent to get away from it all.' He didn't elaborate further, just stared fixedly at the road ahead, locked in his hellish memories for a moment. Sensing he'd said enough, after a rather more amicable silence, it was Lily who steered the subject back to the original, rephrased the question that had annoyed him in the first place.

'So…' Lily said slowly, watching his hands tighten further on the steering-wheel as she spoke, 'were you always this arrogant and confident?'

For a moment he didn't answer, but finally he turned briefly and gave her a very nice smile that promptly melted not just the black atmosphere but another little piece of her heart. 'Always.'

* * *

Leaving behind the last dregs of civilization as they delved further into the wilderness, the winding road bathed in cool green light as the trees canopied overhead, Lily felt a surge of excitement as they neared the house. Hunter turned the car into the overgrown driveway and she turned her head to him and watched his reaction. Watched that haughty, impassive face actually soften as he glimpsed it for the first time.

'It's beautiful, isn't it?' Lily took in the view and as always it was even more beautiful than the last time she'd seen it, a huge rambling white weatherboard home, smothered in wisteria, tall trees behind and to the side, wrapping protective arms around the building, while in front the lush grass gently rolled downwards, drawing the eye to the endless views below.

He didn't answer in words, instead opening the door of the car and climbing out, pulling off his sunglasses and standing stock still.

'I can see how you don't want to lose the place.' Eventually he spoke. 'And I'm the least likely person to be impressed by a view. I rarely set foot out of the city—any city!'

'Because you don't get the time?'

'A bit.' Hunter shrugged. 'And because I've never felt the need. If I need to relax I'll get a massage or…' He didn't finish his sentence, but turned his head towards the house and craned his neck upwards, staring at the mountainside, squinting into the sunlight.

'Come and see inside,' Lily suggested.

'See what I'm buying?'

'I haven't said yes.'

'Yet.'

She didn't respond, just guided him toward the house. Pulling out her keys, she almost tripped over a large picnic basket on the verandah.

'How on earth did this get here?'

'Abigail.' Hunter shrugged. 'I told her to arrange lunch for us.'

'But how did you know the address?' Utterly perplexed, she led the way as he carried the basket and followed her through to the kitchen.

'Mortgagee's auction in Red Hill in two

weeks—that's more than enough information for Abigail.'

'She's efficient, then,' Lily said, giggling a bit as Hunter rolled his eyes.

'So she keeps telling me.' They were wandering through the house, Hunter's knowing eyes taking in every detail as he chatted. 'She wants me to change her job title from Personal Assistant to Personal Secretary and Diary Planner.'

'And what did you say?'

'I didn't say anything—I haven't told you the best bit yet. She didn't *ask!* She actually wrote a letter and—wait for this—she posted it to me. We see each other for twelve sometimes eighteen hours a day and now she's posting me letters! She must have thought I'd take it more seriously if it was a formal request.'

'And did you?' A reluctant smile wobbled on Lily's lips.

'Absolutely. I wrote back to her saying that she can call herself what she bloody well likes so long as she stops hounding me with stupid requests. I suppose I should post it really.'

They were in the study now. Lily flicked on the light, which promptly popped. Despite a bay window it was the one dark room in the place, courtesy of a vast gum tree shadowing the window, but even in the semi-darkness it was beautiful and Lily let out a pensive sigh. 'This is my favourite room—or was.'

She had expected him to move on. Already she'd sensed his restlessness in the bedrooms and realised he was nearing his boredom threshold but, maybe sensing something in her voice, instead of a cursory glance, he came over and wrapped his arms around her, and they stood for a moment in silence, taking in the book-lined walls, the piles of red-gum wood stacked beside the fireplace.

'Was?' It was Hunter who finally broke the heavy silence.

'Dad and I used to spend a lot of time here…' Lily gave a small shrug, kicking herself for giving him an opening. 'When I was studying psychology, I used to be working away at the desk and he'd sit in that recliner…' She pointed to a well-loved leather chair.

'You're a psychologist?'

'Not quite,' Lily corrected. 'I dropped out after my second year.'

'That wasn't very motivated of you,' Hunter admonished, but his teasing tirade halted as he saw the anguish on her features. 'How come?'

'Dad was sick—we needed the money. I did some waitressing and some work at the library—that's how the motivational work-shops started. They had some groups that met and I'd often pop in and listen. One night one of the speakers didn't come so I stepped in and found out I really did have something to say, that I really was good at guiding people with their problems and helping them to set goals. It sort of snowballed from there.'

'You should have gone back and completed your studies.' Hunter was blunt and as Lily looked at him the denial that had been on her lips faded, that tinge of regret for past choices made ebbing as finally she nodded.

'I know,' she said slowly. 'I just…'

'Didn't?'

'Couldn't.' Screwing her eyes closed, she dragged in a deep breath, pain filling her as she glimpsed her past, but she slammed the shutters down in her mind, absolutely refused to go there, instead shaking her head as if to clear it. And when it did, when the memory was gone, when she opened her eyes, everything was OK. Hunter was smiling softly down at her.

'How about lunch?' He let her go then and wandered off, giving her a moment to regroup, to blow her nose and wipe away tears she didn't want him to see from her cheeks. Aware of her reddened eyes and not quite ready to face him, instead she went to the laundry and fished out a fresh light bulb from the cupboard under the sink before heading back to the study.

Aware that if she didn't do it then her mother would, Lily pulled out the heavy desk and balanced the chair rather precariously on top of it. The ceilings were so high in the house that changing a light bulb was a serious balancing act, and one no fifty-year-old woman should attempt! Tucking the new energy-saving bulb in her top, Lily climbed onto the desk and then up onto the chair—one hand firmly on the ceiling for support as the other screwed out the old one. It was a manoeuvre she'd done fifty, maybe a hundred times before, but never with such stunning consequences.

Just as she had screwed it in and was about to climb down, a vice-like grip wrapped around her legs, the chair tumbling over as she was hurled over a pair of very broad, *very* tense shoulders.

'Just what the hell do you think you're doing, Lily?' She was too shocked to answer, the world upside down for a moment till Hunter unceremoniously dumped her on the floor. 'You could have been killed!'

'A heart attack would be more likely!' Lily squealed. 'You scared the life out of me.'

'Why the hell didn't you ask me to do it?' Hunter demanded. 'One slip and you could have broken your neck. Of all the bloody, irresponsible things to do!' He stopped shouting then, raked his hand through his hair, his eyes livid in his pale face as Lily blinked back at him. 'Next time ask for help.'

'Next time,' Lily retorted, smoothing down her skirt and taking a deep breath 'don't interfere.'

CHAPTER SIX

'I COULD stay like this forever.'

Hunter's words caught her by surprise. The argument that Lily felt had blown in from nowhere had disappeared as quickly as it had arrived and they were lying on the picnic blanket, staring up at the blue, blue sky, filled with that dreamy feeling of sleepiness that came from having eaten way too much. And even though it was exactly how Lily was feeling, she'd never expected him to feel the same, had thought that at any moment he'd leap up and start packing up, that the novelty of peace would soon wear off for him. But Hunter wasn't in a rush to go anywhere and, rolling onto her side, propping herself up on her elbow, Lily gazed down at him, saw that unscrupulous face for once relaxed, his eyes closed, his mouth slightly open, and she wanted to reach out and touch him, wanted to press her lips to his.

So she did.

Delivered gently a soft slow kiss, and he let her, didn't move a muscle as she took from him what she wanted, no contact other than their lips, pure unhurried pleasure, like an extra helping of dessert, just because it's there, just because you want it…just because you could.

'Kiss me until I take you again,' Hunter growled as Lily pulled back and smiled at him. She wasn't even shocked by him now—he was so incorrigible, so blatant and unapologetic with his want that he made it more acceptable somehow. He rolled onto his side but only faced her for a second, his eyes moving to her breasts, parting her gaping top and burning her with his gaze. She watched his hand move down to his jeans, saw the bulge of his erection, knew it was for her, a parcel waiting to be opened. A quiver of expectation rippled through her at the goodies that lay ahead, but her smile turned into one of confusion as Hunter pulled an army knife out of the picnic basket, fiddling with all the little instruments and very slowly, very surely selected one, his eyes flashing with pure desire as inched his way over to her.

'What are you doing?' Her voice was thick with lust, not scared, just mounting excitement as he drew the tiny blade towards her.

'Peeling my fruit,' Hunter answered, his warm fingers delving into her cleavage and pulling out the centre of her bra, the blade cutting through the flimsy fabric. He took the weight of her breast as it fell ripe into his hand, taking her nipple in his mouth, kissing it as she had kissed him, unhurriedly, decadently—just because he could. 'Lie down!' His words were a throaty order, and Lily shivered with expectation as she complied. Hunter slowly unzipped her skirt till it was completely open, taking off her shoes till she was wearing only her top and panties, parting her knees. Under any other circumstances she'd have been embarrassed by such exposure, nervous even, yet she didn't feel that way with him in the slightest.

She trusted him.

The admission jolted her.

He was seemingly the most untrustworthy of men and yet somehow she knew better, somehow she knew that in his hands she was safe, that in his own way he actually did care about her.

'I like my new toy.' He was staring down at her, soft dark hair flopping over his forehead, his eyes squinting in concentration, fiddling with that damn army knife again. Lily gave a little gasp as he opened up a tiny pair of scissors, could feel a bubble of moisture welling between her legs, nervous, excited all at the same time.

'This is my favourite set of underwear.'

'I'll buy you some more,' Hunter answered, catching her tentative eyes with his supremely sure ones. 'You're beautiful, Lily.'

She felt it.

Not just in herself but in them. The time spent with him was completely unregrettable, the instincts that had led her to bed with him last night had been so right. And Lily was glad, so glad she'd captured the amazing energy that had engulfed her and gone with it, because today was surely the best of her life and one she'd remember for ever. He was the teacher, showing her herself, the woman inside, and she wanted to learn, wanted to explore with him her body and all its capabilities.

'Do you ever think of going back to your studies?'

He was trimming the silk ribbons that held together her panties with the tiny scissors, and she could only laugh that he could carry on a normal conversation while doing something so incredibly intimate. But it made it easier somehow to answer him, easier to stare up at the sky, feeling the warm sun on her face and his tender hands on her body. She gave in to the moment and revealed a little more of herself.

'Sometimes.' Lily closed her eyes as she thought about it, but Hunter didn't wait for her answer.

'Do you regret giving up?'

'I had no choice,' Lily countered.

'I asked if you regretted it?'

There was the longest silence, Lily's heart thumping in her chest as she admitted what she never had before—even to herself.

'Every single day.'

'Would you do it again?' Hunter pushed. 'I mean, if you could rewind the clock.'

'Don't.' Screwing her eyes closed, Lily tried to block out his words.

'Why don't you go back now?' Hunter's questions were relentless, his instincts spot on.

'I've thought about going back part-time— but I need to work.'

'Not if you marry me!'

His statement forced her eyes open. 'Hunter.' Lily swallowed as her eyes locked with his. 'It couldn't work out.'

'It's only for a year,' Hunter pointed out. 'A year that could change a lot of things for both of us.'

It could. Lily blinked at a future that was financially secure, of saving her mother from the indignity of losing her home—of chasing dreams she had let go for all the wrong reasons. But her wonder turned into a frown of confusion as she stared back at Hunter.

'I just don't get why you need to do this,' Lily attempted, aching for insight into this most complex man. 'I understand Emma's problems, but why does it have to be you fixing them?'

'Because I can,' Hunter said simply, then gave a very wicked smile.

'There has to be more.' Lily tried to continue the conversation, to understand, but the subject was closed. She felt a stirring inside as she looked at him looking at her body with pure lust. 'Pass me your glass.'

'I thought you didn't drink.'

'Sometimes I make exceptions.'

She knew what he was going to do, bracing herself, drenched in arousal, her breath coming in tiny gasps just at the thought of him, watching as he poured the pale liquid, feeling its icy coolness, replaced in a second by his warm tongue, stroking her, making her giddy. Confusion flickered in as he stopped for a moment and it was like they were reading each other's minds, the question answered before it had even been asked.

'There could be so many perfect days, Lily.' Another skilful stroke of his tongue beguiled her as she begged her mind for logic.

'You don't have to sell your home…' Another decadent kiss, his hair tickling her thighs as she quivered in his mouth, tears streaming down her face as emotion ripped through her, her neck arching as he teased her with possibility. She didn't want him to stop, her body begging for him as again he looked up. 'You *can* finish your studies, even work occasionally, have a few one-on-ones *with* your patients in that study.'

Her head tightened as she fought to keep him out, as he crept in and exposed her hidden hopes, unveiled dreams she hadn't even dared envisage. 'You can be everything you want to be, have everything you've ever wanted—if only you say yes.'

He was unzipping his jeans, his potent erection beguiling her.

'I won't last,' he warned, and it didn't matter a scrap because neither would she, yet still he made her wait. Her eyes were wide with arousal as he stroked himself against her, teasing her with the delicious prospects on offer.

'Marry me, Lily.'

He wasn't asking her, he was telling her. A flash of silver told her he was close had her breath bursting in her hot lungs. She wanted him inside her, wanted him beside her—wanted every last thing he could provide.

'Yes.'

She wept the word as he stabbed inside her, her orgasm hitting before he'd even entered, a frantic urgent coupling that had them both dizzy, the sweet, sweet sensation of him spilling inside her as once again Hunter got his wicked way.

CHAPTER SEVEN

THE cool feeling of the gold as he pushed the ring on her finger confused her.

Her signature on a piece of paper was such a paltry summing up of what was taking place and she wanted to call an urgent halt, to tell the magistrate that he didn't love her, but as she took the pen Lily knew it didn't matter a scrap.

Legally they were husband and wife.

He kissed her over and over, kissed her for the sake of her family, who were enthralled by the romance of it all, for the press that were duly gathered and for the duties in life that were ever present, confusion building with each sip of champagne, each offer of congratulations. Hunter was so absolutely convincing, so elegant and charming that at times Lily almost felt as if it were real, almost relaxed and enjoyed herself, but it only compounded her misery when reality hit.

Arranging a hasty wedding was absolutely no problem when you had an open chequebook and Hunter Myles was the groom. The formalities had been followed by the most tasteful of receptions at an exclusive five-star hotel and the whole day had run so smoothly it was as if the wedding had been months in the making. Every detail had been taken care of, from the stunning white-gold diamond solitaire on her finger right down to Emma playing the violin for them as the bride and groom took to the floor, the strains of music so emotive, so beautiful that as Hunter held her close, as she leant her exhausted head against his chest and closed her eyes, inhaled his scent as he gracefully led, it was so easy to lose herself to the fantasy that everyone believed, that love had raced in and swept them to this moment.

'You look amazing.' Hunter pulled her closer, lowered his head so that his mouth was by her ear, his breath caressing her as he spoke. 'You *feel* amazing.' She didn't answer, just let his words sweep over her, wished that Emma would play on for ever, that somehow this dance would never end. 'Today's been perfect, I'm so proud...'

'Don't.' Her eyes snapped open, stiffening in his arms. Losing the rhythm of the music, she tripped slightly, but Hunter steadied her, held her tighter as she struggled to keep up, the fantasy, the moment doused because he'd taken it too far, spoken to her with the tenderness of a real groom on his wedding day. 'Don't pretend that it's real.'

'But it is, Lily' His deep voice was back in her ear, lulling her back to the rhythm again. 'You *are* beautiful and I *am* proud to be here with you, so stop fighting it.' His lips were grazing her cheek as her eyes fluttered closed until softly his mouth found hers—kissing her back to safety, quelling her protests, her fears before releasing her from the haven of his arms. And Hunter was right. It was easier to stop fighting it, to be beautiful and proud for as long as it could last, so for the rest of dance she gave in, allowed herself the luxury of the moment that was theirs.

As the music finished the dancers stopped to applaud and Lily stared in awe at his sister, full of admiration for her talent because, quite simply, she'd never heard anything so beautiful—or seen someone shine so much as they played—the violin was almost an extension of Emma, the emotion coursing through her and out through the instrument. 'She plays beautifully,' Lily commented, but Hunter wasn't listening, a frown on his darkening face as he peered across the room.

'Who's that lech talking to her?' Hunter's voice had a very proprietorial ring to it but Lily laughed as she followed his gaze and saw who Emma was talking to.

'That's my cousin, Jim, and he's certainly not a lech—he's delightful.'

'He's all over her.' Hunter's voice was clipped. 'What the hell's he doing?'

'Talking to her,' Lily said calmly. 'It looks as if he's bought her a drink and now he's talking to her.'

'Mauling her more like.'

'They're flirting.' Lily dragged him round to face her. 'That's what single people do!'

'But she's—'

'She's twenty-five,' Lily cut in, feeling his protectiveness for his sister and understanding it, 'and she's very beautiful and very talented.'

Her words seemed to reach him, the tension leaving his face. Perhaps realising he was over-reacting, he gave Lily a smile as her mother walked over, congratulating them both for the hundredth time and commenting on Emma's spectacular performance.

'She wanted to play for us.' Hunter smiled. 'I so glad you're enjoying yourself, Mrs Harper— I mean, Catherine.'

'How could I not?' Catherine beamed. 'Though if anyone had told me a couple of weeks ago I'd be at Lily's wedding today, I'd have said they were mad. I can't believe the speed of it all.'

'Neither can we!' Hunter suitably answered. 'But we figured why wait when you know something's right?'

'And it *is* right.' Catherine nodded earnestly. 'I have to admit when Lily told me what was happening I had my doubts, but seeing the two of you together has completely put my mind at ease—I can just tell you adore each other.' From the squeeze of his hand on her waist, no doubt Hunter thought her mother's mind had been soothed by her new son-in-law's rather impressive prerequisites, but Lily knew better and she would tell Hunter so later. 'I *know* you're going to be happy together—I just know it, darling.' Her hand reached for her daughter's face, holding it for a moment. Lily knew what was coming next and closed her eyes to keep the tears in. 'Your father would be so proud of you today.'

Hunters grip on her thankfully tightened, no doubt feeling the depth of emotion that coursed through her as her mother spoke on. 'Lily and her father are incredibly close,' Catherine explained to Hunter, slipping from past to present tense. Lily felt Hunter's beat of tension sear through her body, realised he'd heard the mistake, too, but thankfully his smile didn't change. 'He was a wonderful man. If you and Lily can experience just a fraction of the love we share, you'll be doing well.'

'You must miss him terribly,' the new perfect son-in-law murmured, but Catherine shook her head.

'Why would I miss him when I know that he's still with me?'

'Are you OK?' For once he wasn't superior or mocking, for once his question was straightforward and genuine, which made it all the harder to answer. A quick retort would be so much easier than opening up the most painful part of her.

'I'm fine,' Lily said, then bit hard on her lip and turned her head so he couldn't see her face. But Hunter was having none of it. Taking her by the hand, he led her outside onto the balcony and she went without resistance. Only when she was outside did she realise how much tension was stringing her together, how much she'd actually needed some space to be able to drop the charade for just a couple of moments.

'It's just been a long day.' Lily dragged in the cool night air, tried to make light of her threatening tears. 'Hormones, perhaps.'

'Well, according to my girl user manual…' he drew out a tiny smile from her as he refused to be fobbed off '…the P in PMT is definitely pre- and not post-menstrual tension!'

Trust him to remember—the moment of panic when they'd realised they hadn't used contraception had been countered almost immediately by Lily's period and she'd gone straight on the Pill, which to Hunter's delight had, in two weeks, added a cup size to her breasts.

'And don't blame the Pill!' Hunter said, reading her mind.

'I can blame whatever I want,' Lily answered tartly. 'And if you'd read the next chapter of your girly user manual, it would have told you that thanks to the Pill, I'm feeling bloated and nauseous.'

'I must have skipped that part.' He pulled her back towards him. 'Come on, Lily, what's really wrong?' He wasn't going to give in, so Lily gave him some of what he was demanding, told him a just a little of how she was feeling.

'I just feel like a fraud in there—pretending to be happy.'

'But, why wouldn't you be happy?' Hunter asked, bemused. 'I'm happy.'

'How?' She stared back at him. 'How can you be happy when you're fooling everyone?'

'Because we're not.' He shook his head. 'And unlike a lot of couples on their wedding day, we're not fooling ourselves either. We both like and respect each other. We're both going to do everything we can to make this the best marriage—even if it is finite. Just because it has a use-by date, it doesn't mean it can't be good and productive.'

'I guess.' Lily nodded, wishing she could be comforted, but each word cut like a knife because each word spelt out the inevitable end.

'I don't think that's all that's upsetting you, though,' Hunter said, and her stomach tightened. 'Is it what your mother said about your father?'

'Leave it.' She shook her head, her resolve not to cry weakening.

He noticed, his warm thumb absorbing a mascara-laced tear before it even fell. 'I know how you feel, Lily.'

'No, Hunter.' She shook her head. 'You don't.'

'I lost my parents last year,' Hunter pointed out, perhaps to elicit sympathy, perhaps to show that he really did understand, but Lily knew that there was no way he could, no way he could know the pain her mother's words had evoked, the utter wretchedness of being privy to a secret you wished you'd never found out. 'You'll never understand how I feel.'

'Try me,' Hunter offered, but again she shook her head. His wife she may be, but her emotions, her secrets were hers. She still owned herself and no piece of paper, no amount of money could ever change that.

'I'm going to go and freshen up.' She pushed

him away, pushed him away because if she spent another second in his arms, she'd tell him her pain, let him in on the secret she's sworn she'd never reveal. And she was truly scared at how much she wanted to. 'I'll meet you back in there.'

It was a relief to be alone, to close a heavy door on the revelry of the wedding and mute the sounds to more manageable proportions, to stare at her reflection in the mirror and somehow attempt to find herself, to gather up the strewn emotions and arrange them in a semblance of order. Only it wasn't going to happen tonight! Somehow she managed a smile as a very good-looking woman came in and joined her at the mirror, catching Lily's eyes as she leant forward in the mirror and checked her expertly made-up face.

'Enjoying yourself?' Her voice was as expensive as her outfit and Lily tried to place her, but realised they hadn't been introduced because she certainly wasn't someone you'd forget in hurry—black, glossy hair rippled down olive shoulders, her tall, elegant frame exquisitely draped in a silver sheath of a dress. And even though it was her own wedding, the bride felt rather drab in comparison, especially when the stunning creature proceeded to rearrange her ample cleavage.

'Immensely.' Lily gave what she hoped was a suitable response. 'I don't think we were introduced.'

'We weren't!' Gold eyes caught Lily's and held them. 'I was too busy working. I'm the one who organised this wedding. I'm the one you have to thank for your *immensely* enjoyable day!'

Stunning she might be, but she had that raw, dangerous glint in her eyes of a woman suffering the wounds of a recent break-up, and at that moment Lily realised who she was dealing with—the woman Hunter had declared was well and truly over him!

Thanks a lot, Hunter, Lily inwardly groaned as she mustered all her people skills to deal with this rather uncomfortable situation. 'You must be Abigail,' Lily attempted, trying to defuse this rather volatile situation. 'Hunter speaks very highly of you and I can see why. You've done an amazing job. Thank you.'

'Oh, it's far more than a *job*.' Abigail's face was dangerously close, so close Lily could smell the excess champagne on her breath, could *feel* the hatred and anger coursing from her livid body. 'I assume you're expecting me to offer my congratulations?'

'After these last few weeks I've learned never to assume anything,' Lily answered, declining the rather provocative question and instead attempting to end things. But Abigail had clearly waited for this moment, had no doubt spent the last weeks planning not just the wedding but the confrontation, too, and Lily realised with an inward sigh unless she was willing to push past her and make a rapid exit from the ladies' room, she didn't have much option other than to let Abigail have her angry say.

'Hunter's incapable of remaining faithful for five minutes. Trust me, I know.'

'Thanks for the warning,' Lily responded

tightly, glancing at the door and wishing someone—*anyone*—would come in.

'Don't turn your back for a second, *Mrs Myles,* because if it isn't me then I can guarantee there will be someone else willing and waiting.'

'Feel free,' Lily answered, 'but know you're in for one helluva wait—I happen to trust my husband.'

'Then you're a fool.' Abigail spat, tossing her hair and walking out.

'Everything OK?' Hunter dutifully kissed Lily on the cheek for the benefit of the onlookers as she made her way over, still shaking slightly from the confrontation. 'What took you so long?'

'I just ran into one of your psycho ex-girlfriends in the ladies' room.' Smiling sweetly, she whispered into his ear, 'Thanks for the warning!' But if she'd expected contrition she didn't get it, Hunter's face breaking into a grin as he swept her onto the dance floor.

'Who was it?'

That he didn't even know who it might be

should have made things worse but, despite herself, there was a sliver of a smile on her face at his appalling question. He was so utterly and completely bad, but so impossibly divine. 'For future reference, that was the wrong response, Hunter!'

'I never said I didn't have a past.'

'Did you have to bring it to the wedding?' Lily quipped.

'Come on. Who was it?'

She nearly told him, even opened her mouth to answer him, but at the last moment thought better of it, recalling the old saying of keeping friends close and enemies closer, realising there and then she'd need to keep her wits about her to play this game and survive.

'It doesn't matter who it was,' Lily answered, her eyes suddenly serious, the teasing note in her voice completely gone as she stared back at him. 'The fact is I told her that I trusted my husband, so don't make me a fool here, Hunter. Know that I don't give out second chances.'

'I won't need one.'

And he said it so confidently, so assuredly, pulled her so close as they danced that for now she chose to believe him. Lily closed her eyes on the world that was watching them, waiting for them to slip up, waiting for them to fall, and just let Hunter hold her.

CHAPTER EIGHT

'THIS,' said Hunter, pushing open a vast navy door and stepping aside to let her through, 'is home.'

For now.

He didn't say it but she felt the two words hanging in the air, felt again the transient nature of her existence for the next twelve months.

Stepping into Hunter's vast apartment, Lily tried and failed not to be daunted by the expensive surroundings of his exclusive penthouse. His apartment, *their* apartment, took up the entire top floor of the high-rise city building, the shimmering city skyline visible not through a window but an entire glassed wall, like some scenic lookout making her slightly giddy as she neared it, as if she were standing on the edge of some unstable precipice, as if with one slip, one misplaced move she'd topple out into the vast night sky.

'Do you want a tour?' Hunter asked, picking up a remote and flicking on some music, but Lily shook her head.

'I'll just have a wander around, if you don't mind.'

Which she did. Wide-eyed, she took in the luxuriously expensive surroundings. The music Hunter had turned on was piped into every tastefully furnished room, and though it was undoubtedly the most exclusive opulent residence she had ever set foot inside, not for a second could it be considered a home. There was nothing 'lived in' about it, nothing that truly denoted Hunter. He hadn't chosen the tasteful paintings that hung on the orchid-white walls or the bed-linen that was pulled taut on the vast king-size bed—somehow instinctively she knew that. It was like visiting a display home or checking into a luxury hotel, Lily thought as she pushed open a door. The marble bathroom gleamed, the toilet paper folded into a neat little V shape, shampoo and conditioner bottles full and perfectly positioned. She half expected a 'cleaned and sealed' sign to have been placed on the lavatory. Wandering through to the kitchen it was much the same there—sparkling stainless-steel appliances that were surely never used. As Hunter joined her she pulled open the fridge and peered inside at the minimal contents—some dips and wine, a cheese platter with fruit and a jug of cream, all no doubt checked and replenished by the cleaner each morning.

'I tend to eat out,' Hunter offered by way of explanation, 'or if you want to eat in ring down to the doorkeeper and he'll arrange for one of one of the local restaurants to deliver.'

'We could even try cooking something!' Lily responded, but the sarcasm was completely wasted on him and Lily tried to shrug of her unease with a smile as they made their way back into the lounge. 'Your apartment's stunning.'

'Really.' Hunter sounded surprised that she

liked it. 'The stereo system's great, I guess, but…' he stared around for a moment '…it's a bit bland, don't you think? And I hate those bloody paintings, especially that one.' He jabbed a finger towards the offending article. 'Ten grand for a bloody triangle on top of a circle.'

'Why did you get it, then?' Lily asked, laughing at his indignation.

'The interior designer chose it.' Hunter put on an effeminate voice. *'To provide a soothing focal point.'*

She was only half listening, staring now out of the glass wall into the night.

The most beautiful man she had ever seen, the most complex, engaging of characters was hers to explore, to adore, to be with, and as if sensing her thoughts he crossed the room and stood behind her, wrapping his arms loosely around her waist. He leaned slightly on her shoulder as he pressed his cheek against hers and gazed out at into the night, watching the birds swirling around the lights of the Arts

Centre, the noisy, vibrant city of Melbourne, silent through the thick glass.

'My sister liked you.' Hunter's low voice bought her out of her daydream and Lily smiled as she leant back into him.

'I liked her, though she's nothing like I imagined.'

'In what way?'

'I just expected…' Lily bit her tongue, her choice of words perhaps a touch harsh, but from the way Hunter had described his sister Lily had been expecting a bitter, depressed woman, one struggling to come to terms with her injuries. Yet Emma had appeared anything but—her smile was infectious, her sheer joy and passion for life blatant. She was either a brilliant actress or…Lily frowned, unseen by Hunter, confused at the lack of alternatives on offer.

'Your mum's great!' Hunter gave a low laugh.

'You mean she's as mad as a cut snake.' Lily gave a small giggle of her own. 'She talks about Dad as if he's just popped over to the bar and will back any minute. It used to worry me, now I just smile.'

'I still don't get it.' Hunter's grip tightened on her, as if sensing that she'd wriggle away, and he was right, because the second he broached the subject Lily tensed. If his arms hadn't been firmly holding her, she'd surely have walked away. 'If you'd had my parents I'd understand your views on love being a bit jaded, but your mum and dad were clearly devoted to each other. Surely, even after what happened with Mark, you'd have a little more faith!'

But, for Lily, more surprising than his insight was that for the first time she wanted to talk about it, actually wanted to share with Hunter a bit of the loneliness she was feeling.

Even if this marriage was devoid of love, there was still closeness, and maybe it would help, maybe telling him what was eating at her now would ease a fraction of her troubled mind.

'I always thought they *were* devoted to each other—my childhood was pretty much perfect, I guess.' She was watching a train far below pull into the station, like a movie with the sound turned off, and somehow it was easier to focus on the lives on the streets below than what she was saying. 'Mum and Dad were great. Even when I was a teenager I still got on well with them, not like some of my friends…'

'No rebellion years?'

'There was nothing to rebel against,' Lily answered pensively. 'I truly thought we were all OK.'

His arms tightened around her and she leant back on him, glad of his strength, his solid warmth, grateful, so grateful that he didn't push her to go on, seemed to understand how hard it was to reveal.

'This isn't just about your father dying, is it?' he said softly as she crumpled. 'Tell me, Lily.'

'I don't want to,' she whispered. Only somehow she did. Gulping, tentative she told out her story. 'Just before he died, Mum got it into her head that she wanted to show him some photos. She sent me up to the attic…'

'Go on,' Hunter said, and now he was

pushing, but Lily was glad to have someone guiding her through this minefield of emotion, glad to have someone strong and assured to cling to as she crept tentatively on. 'I was in the attic, sorting out old boxes and suitcases. I found some letters.' She wasn't crying any more. Her voice was bitter, her words tainted as she lived again the vileness of her discovery. 'Some from *him,* some from *her.*' Pale lips snarled the words, and Hunter's expression told her that finally he understood. 'It wasn't just a brief fling.' She answered what hadn't even been asked, ticked of the list of questions that she'd asked herself back then. 'It went on for two years. I'd have been about twelve when it started. It was pretty intense…'

'You read them all?'

'All of them,' She nodded, closing her eyes as the torrid words that had been penned all those years ago seemed to dance in her vision. 'And then I burnt them.'

'Did you tell your mum?'

'How?' Lily asked, tears starting again,

hysteria creeping into her voice. 'I raced round to Mark. I wanted him to tell me what to do…'

'And you found out that the whole world had gone mad,' Hunter offered. In spite of herself Lily gave a watery grin at his description. When she'd found Mark with Janey it had felt *exactly* as if her world had gone mad. 'I just couldn't tell Mum—I'd have taken away her whole life if I'd told her, taken away all her memories. How could I tell her it was all just a sham, that the man she loved, adored right till the very end, had been cheating on her?'

'You couldn't,' Hunter said very firmly, very clearly, and it helped, helped that he concurred, that that awful, painful decision she'd made had surely been the right one. 'You could never have told her that.'

'I wish I'd never found them,' she whispered. 'I wish I'd never given my career up for a man who was nothing more than a cheat, I wish I'd never found out the truth.'

'But you don't know the truth, Lily.' His words confused her and she frowned up at him.

'You think you found it in those letters, but that's only a fraction of it. He was still a great father and, despite what you found, he was still a great husband.'

'He was a cheat!'

'He was human, Lily. It's not your secret to keep or reveal.'

'I don't understand.'

'You probably never will,' Hunter said softly. 'So let it go.'

'It's not that easy…' She was quarrelling more with herself than with him because she wanted it to be the case, wanted to be able to put the truth she'd discovered aside, but she just couldn't.

'Let him be your dad again, Lily.' He took the biggest problem in her life to date and shrank it as if by magic, folded up the impossible, complicated map she'd been trying and failing to follow and tossed it aside, offering her a far easier path to follow. 'Don't try to work it all out.'

'Is that what you do?' She blinked at him. 'Just refuse to go there?'

'Where?'

'Inside yourself.'

'There's nothing lurking there. I deal with things as they happen—and then I move on.'

'No.' Boldly she confronted him. She'd given so much of herself it was as if she wanted a piece of him in return—a piece of his soul that she could keep for ever—no matter what the future held for them. 'Hunter, maybe you didn't have the greatest relationship with them, but they were your parents and with all that's happened to your sister…'

'Lily.' He shook his head, smiled at her almost with pity that she couldn't quite get it. 'It happened—and beating myself up over it isn't going to change a single thing.'

'What happened?' Boldly she stared at him, pushed for details because she needed them. 'Hunter, it's just so recent. What happened was so awful—surely there must be some unresolved—'

'Oh, please!' Hunter just rolled his eyes. 'Don't start with your psychobabble.'

'I know about your parents, what happened to Emma—were you involved?'

'Nope.' He gave a thin smile. 'So no *unresolved* guilt there. Yes, it was bloody, yes, it was awful, the police coming to the door isn't a particularly pleasant memory, that I'm prepared to admit. However, beating myself on the chest isn't going to change things—going over and over the hows and whys isn't going to turn back the clock.'

'I guess…but…'

'Leave it,' he snapped, then regretted his harshness; there was something in her voice that twisted his stomach, something he hadn't heard when he'd been sitting on the couch at New Beginnings. Far, far more than professional interest, those knowing curious eyes blazing with concern. And for Hunter, instead of reassuring him, it actually terrified him—not that she couldn't possibly understand.

More the fact that she just might.

That in revealing his pain, he might also reveal his fears.

For her.

It was more than a beat of hesitation, wrenching indecision hanging in the air as patiently she waited—offered without words this step towards intimacy.

Offered herself to the lions, Hunter thought with sickening realisation—a future like his past, like his mother's past.

'No buts!' he said more softly, smiled that devilish smile and promptly diverted the conversation, dragged her closer physically as he pushed her away emotionally. 'We've got more important things to attend to now.'

'Like what?'

'Like consummating this marriage.'

'Hunter…' She opened her mouth to protest, wanted so badly for him to talk to her, to reveal a bit more of himself to her, but, as always, when she ventured too far into his guarded thoughts Hunter shot her away with a silver bullet.

'No arguments,' he said softly. 'You're my wife now and you'll do as I say.'

'Joking,' he added, as Lily stiffened in his arms, her eyes narrowing at his choice of words.

'Well, it wasn't very funny,' Lily responded. 'Because if you think—' He didn't let her finish, stopping her protest with his mouth. But nothing, not even his skilful kisses, could completely hush the incessant voice that told her Hunter hadn't been joking. Nothing, not even the mastery of his touch, could completely obliterate the troubled thoughts that tumbled through her mind.

That by stepping into Hunter's world, by becoming his wife, somehow she'd lost control. That no matter how willing a participant she was in this relationship, it was Hunter calling all the shots.

CHAPTER NINE

'SHOULD we go to Emma's dressing room and wish her luck?' Clutching a glass of champagne, hemmed in by the masses having a pre-performance drink, Lily suddenly felt claustrophobic.

'Why?' Hunter shot her a cool stare. Since he'd come from work he'd been at his bloodiest, snapping for her to hurry up and get ready then proceeding to spend half an hour on his phone to Abigail as Lily stood, dressed to the nines, waiting to leave for Emma's return to the stage.

'How was work?' Hunter asked, a seemingly normal question, but with indescribable connotations. Her need to assert herself, to keep a link with her temporary past and inevitable future was a niggling bone of contention.

'Difficult,' Lily bristled. 'It's hard, showing you can relate to people when you arrive in a chauffer-driven car.'

'Don't go, then.' Hunter shrugged, deliberately missing the point. She *wanted* to work, *wanted* to keep that part of herself that was so vital to her soul. No matter how big the donation Hunter had made for the centre she worked at, no matter how easy it would be for them to find another counsellor, hell, maybe even a *real* psychologist now—still it didn't sit right with Lily, and no matter how many times she attempted to explain, quite simply Hunter didn't get it. But she knew with certainty that he didn't need to be quite so poisonous.

He was undoubtedly nervous, Lily told herself. Emma's return to performing was such a momentous leap that it wasn't any wonder he was on edge—but Hunter on edge was like no other. In fact, Lily decided, marriage to Hunter was like struggling through a thesaurus without a dictionary.

Easy to describe—impossible to define.

In the weeks since their wedding, every emotion in her had been triggered—every second spent with Hunter a roller-coaster ride—intoxicating highs, followed by devastating lows. His easy wit, his engaging company, his voracious appetite for sex countered with black moods that no longer blew in from nowhere. Instead, they were tiny whirlwinds that danced endlessly on the horizon, merging unpredictably, and each time their impact was more devastating.

'Anyway.' Hunter reverted back to the original topic. 'The dressing room's no doubt a bit crowded. Your cousin Jim's down with her, no doubt fawning all over her.'

'Good,' Lily shot back. 'She deserves a bit of tenderness.'

He didn't reply, the ringing of his phone beating the undoubted barb on the tip of his tongue, and Lily felt her own teeth grinding together as Abigail somehow managed to invade yet again. Hunter turned his wide shoulders on the crowd to take the call as Lily took a sip from her glass, and promptly felt as if she might throw it up, the crowd, the heavy clash of perfumes, the rather toxic atmosphere all combining to make her feel thoroughly miserable.

'What's wrong?' Hunter asked when finally the call ended and the bell went for everyone to take their seats.

'I'm just a bit hot.'

'That was just Abigail, confirming that Emma's flowers had been delivered—if that's what's worrying you.'

'It isn't.' Lily shook her head and wished she hadn't. The room was spinning mercilessly, not that Hunter noticed. He was taking her arm to guide her in as the crowed surged forward, and for an appalling moment Lily thought she might pass out, right there in front of everyone, and, worse still, right there in front of Hunter. 'I'm just going to the ladies' room.'

Which was easier said than done. Hunter's irritated curse rang in her ears as she went against the tide, black suits and bow-ties blurring like a hypnotic wheel as she stumbled towards the ladies' and sat, undignified in a thousand-dollar gown, on the loo seat lid with her head down between her knees, the stifling heat replaced now with an icy chill, a cold sweat drenching her.

'Please, please, stop,' Lily demanded of the universe, knowing that Hunter was outside, knowing how huge this moment was for Emma, for him. Desperate not to spoil it, she licked her dry lips in relief as slowly everything came back into focus, her heart rate slowing down, the blood that had drained out of her face making a slow but steady return till finally, gingerly, she sat up.

It was the rich food, Lily told herself, running her wrists under the tap and rinsing her mouth before reapplying her lipstick—the endless late nights and even more frequent early morning awakenings, courtesy of Hunter's almost permanent erection.

She even managed a small grin in the mirror before heading back out to face him and no doubt another sarcastic barb, but, surprisingly he didn't say anything, just took her arm and this time led them to their seats without incident, his body absolutely rigid beside her. Shooting a glance at him just before the lights dimmed, Lily saw his taut features, the grim set of his jaw and knew he was terrified for Emma, knew somehow that his vileness tonight was more about him than her.

'She'll be OK,' Lily offered softly, putting a hand over his tense one and, whether he wanted it or not, holding it.

'Will she?'

Even in the darkness she could see the anguish in his eyes as he turned to her for a moment and Lily could have wept for him. She knew somehow that the guilt he so vehemently denied was sitting right there between them.

'She'll be great!'

Oh, and she was.

For the first part of the performance they sat on tenterhooks, waiting for her solo, the exquisite music far from soothing because Emma had to match it—better it even—and when finally it was her turn, as the lights dimmed for a moment, as Emma took her place on the stage, Lily felt Hunter's hand tighten around hers and could have sworn they both stopped breathing, knowing Emma was moving out of her wheelchair. Every muscle in Hunter was taut until finally the clearest, purest of notes filled the packed theatre, Emma, exquisite at centre stage. Her jet hair streamed down her slender shoulders, her black ballgown merging into the elegant chair, but it wasn't the absence of the wheelchair that rendered her disability to diminishable proportions. It was Emma herself— her talent, her elegance, her sheer presence that had the entire audience captivated till the last note died away, applause thundering as they leapt to their feet in an impromptu standing ovation, only Hunter a step behind everyone, Hunter with an expression Lily couldn't quite read on his face as he stared down to the stage and his sister. Lily would have given *anything* to know what he was thinking.

Anything to know what really moved this man.

Anything for him.

The rest of the show was agony—Hunter, bored now, just wanted it over to congratulate Emma, Lily shrinking into her chair, wishing the room would quiet for just a moment so she could counter the impossible thought that had occurred to her.

Love—true love—didn't exist. Lily knew that, knew that, knew that. In the worst possible way she'd found out the truth, had been betrayed not just by her fiancé but by her father. The fact that true love was impossible was the single reason she was here, safe in the knowledge that it couldn't last, playing the game for each other's gain.

And yet…

The lights blazing on snapped her out of her introspection. Hunter was the first in the theatre standing, and Lily stared up, blushing and suddenly shy.

'Come on!' he growled, snapping his impatient fingers for her to follow him, and Lily was actually grateful for his arrogance, grateful for his pompous demeanour…glad that her moment of stupidity was over, because how, Lily questioned, following his wide shoulders as he rudely, without apology, bumped knees and trampled programmes in his haste to get out, could anyone love that?

'You were great, Em!' Backstage and completely ignoring Jim, who was holding Emma's hand, Hunter gave his sister a congratulatory hug.

'Just like old times, huh?' Emma asked questioningly, and Lily felt a shiver run up her spine as she saw Hunter's eyes flick to the wheelchair and back, saw the agony etched in his face as he attempted a terse nod.

'Easily as good as before!'

'Better,' Emma said softly, her hand still coiled around Jim's, her face glowing. 'I'm playing better than before.'

'How?' Hunter frowned. 'I mean, all the trouble you've had with balance…'

'I've worked that out now.' Emma was almost tripping over her words in her joy. 'I can't explain it. It's as if all the pain, all I've been through is there, right there in my music, as if everything I can't say I can…'

'Play…' Lily offered, smiling as Emma gave a grateful nod. 'You were fantastic. I know nothing about music, but I do know you were amazing.'

'Thanks, Lily.' They'd clicked at the wedding and Emma often called around at the apartment or met Lily for coffee, bolstering Lily's confidence when an unflattering photo of her appeared in a magazine, laughing out loud at some of the hurtful comments—the press delighting in calling her a nobody and questioning how someone so apparently *plain* could seemingly have captured Hunter's heart.

'How about dinner, then?' Hunter suggested, but his voice faded into a frown as Emma shook her head.

'Jim's already booked a table. For two,' she added, wincing as she did so.

'Well, we'll tell them to make it for four,' Hunter clipped, but, seeing Emma's blush, Lily leapt to her rescue.

'Actually, I'm exhausted, Hunter. I really

could do with just going home and going to bed. You don't mind, do you?' Lily needlessly checked with Emma, giving a tiny unseen wink as Emma gave a relieved shake of her head.

'Of course not.' Emma smiled as Hunter stalked out with barely a goodbye. 'Thanks so much for coming and for the gorgeous flowers… Oh and, Lily…' As she made to go and catch up with her impossible husband, the whisper of anguish in Emma's voice had Lily turning around. 'I don't want to tell you how to…' Her eyes pleaded for Lily's permission to go on, but a bewildered Lily just stared. 'You know this is *so* hard for him.'

Only she didn't—didn't know because Hunter refused over and over to tell her what was going on inside. At every turn he thwarted her, at every attempt he pushed her away. Only how could she tell Emma that? How could she tell this gorgeous, vibrant woman that the brother she so dearly loved, that the marriage she so clearly endorsed were both a sham.

'Surely it's harder for you?' Lily answered

carefully, hoping for a flash of clarity, but instead the waters muddied further as Emma slowly, so slowly, shook her head.

'Lily, just keep telling him that none of this is his fault—one day he'll hopefully believe it.'

'What was that about?' Hunter asked, tapping an impatient foot as his driver flashed his lights from the traffic lights to tell him he was coming. 'Emma wanted—'

'To be alone with Jim,' Lily broke in. 'Only you're too insensitive to see it.'

'Hell!' As his driver pulled up at the kerb, it was as if the anger, the tension in him just dissipated, a smile creeping onto his face as an impossible thought occurred. 'Do you realise,' he said out of the corner of his mouth, 'that if they end up getting married, my ex-wife could be at the wedding.'

'My ex-husband, too.' Lily gave a rather more wobbly smile, still bristling at his impossible behavior tonight, still reeling at the impossible thought that had earlier occurred to her and still utterly bemused by whatever it was Emma had been trying to tell her.

'Your cousin and my sister…' Hunter mused. 'Would that make us related?'

'Heaven help us!' Lily dry response actually made him laugh, and then totally unashamedly, despite the crowd outside the concert hall, despite traffic piling up behind his silver car, Hunter pulled her into his arms and gave her the most thorough of kisses.

Or because of them? Lily wondered as a camera flashed. She pulled back, slightly breathless from the intensity of his kiss and suddenly felt more than a bit used.

'Was that for the cameras?' Lily asked. But Hunter shook his head, that gorgeous, debauched mouth moving in on hers once again, those strong warm hands on her bare back, as her insides promptly melted.

'That—' Hunter's voice was low and very definite '—was for me!'

CHAPTER TEN

'ARE you doing anything today?'

He knotted his tie as he spoke, standing proud and beautiful amid a pile of damp towels and the chaos of a man who neither cared nor needed to pick up after himself.

'I'm not sure.' Lily yawned and stretched, blinking at the day that lay ahead of her, realising it was the first time since she'd met Hunter that she had a whole day to do with whatever she wished. The haste of their marriage should had left an endless ream of loose ends to tie up, juggling work and playing the part of Hunter's wife two ridiculous parallels, listening and working on people's problems while seemingly having escaped from hers. And, admittedly, the glamorous world she had stepped into had been immense fun at first—lining her wardrobe with designer clothes, having her blonde hair styled and *maintained,* not just at the most exclusive of salons but by the owner himself. But she felt as if she were living on a movie set, only one where the cameras never stopped rolling, playing the part of Hunter's wife impinging more and more on her real world, Hunter's leading lady, seemingly an all-consuming role.

'Actually, no.' Lily grinned at the prospect of a free day. 'I might go and look for a car. The mechanic said it would be cheaper to replace my old one than repair it properly.' Lily saw his hands still for a second, the tie he was looping pausing midway, and Lily felt herself stiffen in defence. 'I'm not expecting you to pay for it!' Even though she'd been desperately trying to help fund a huge mortgage for her mother, Lily hadn't exactly been derelict financially when she met him—and she certainly wasn't expecting Hunter to dangle a keyring to some sleek sports car, but still he shook his head.

'What's wrong with Lachlan?' Hunter

asked, referring to the driver Abigail had arranged for her.

'Nothing.' Lily frowned.

'Because if you're not happy with him, I can ask Abigail to—'

'You don't need to ask Abigail to do anything on my behalf,' Lily interrupted, sitting up in bed, irritated that something so straightforward was being made so needlessly complicated. 'Lachlan's perfectly fine. I just can't stand being driven everywhere when I'm more than capable of driving myself.'

'But there's no need.' Hunter wasn't listening. Instead he was loading up his briefcase with various papers and filling up his suit pockets with his mobile phone and wallet, deliberately ignoring her protests. When Lily raised her voice a touch to get his attention Hunter just switched the subject. 'Just forget about looking for a car—why don't we meet for lunch?'

'Are you going to ask Abigail to pencil me in?' Lily asked nastily. Every minute of his exhausting day was planned and accounted for by the ever-efficient, seemingly ever-present Abigail. It was as if Abigail's emotional outburst at the wedding had never happened. Blasé and bold, she strode into the apartment in the mornings, treating Lily with nothing more than polite boredom, as if she was just another of her boss's details to arrange, as she went through Hunter's schedule with him, which was no mean feat—he could be in Sydney in the morning, Melbourne in the after-noon and checking in at the international depar-tures lounge of the airport by evening for a three-day trip to Singapore. But no matter how indispensable Abigail was, no matter how pro-fessional she appeared with Hunter, Lily neither trusted nor liked her. 'I don't want to meet for lunch. I want to go and look at a car.'

'It's not open for discussion, Lily.' Only now did he look at her, his stance completely im-movable. 'Abigail's had practically every magazine in Australia's features editor trying to arrange an interview—the press still have their lenses trained on you, trying to get a hint of a pregnancy bump.'

'A pregnancy bump?' Lily gave a shocked laugh. 'What are you talking about?'

'That's the reason for most hasty marriages.' Hunter gave a little shudder. 'Heaven forbid. But, like it or not, it's hard enough to explain why you insist on working, but the sight of you in a secondhand car yard isn't exactly going to douse their interest.'

What Hunter was saying did make sense— the interest from *everyone* had unsettled and shocked her to say the least. Hunter Myles, as she'd found out from the evening news the night before her wedding, wasn't just gorgeous in her eyes—he was one of Australia's top most eligible bachelors, or had been. His hasty marriage had caused more than a stir of interest. But even if it made perfect sense she felt uneasy, felt another piece of her freedom being chipped away—yet another price to pay that Lily hadn't considered when she'd agreed to this marriage.

'I'll leave it for today, then,' she reluctantly agreed.

'Good girl.' Clearly happy he'd got his way, he sat on the bed, took her hands and toyed with them until they relaxed a touch then kissed away the frown that was forming on her face.

'But only until things have calmed down,' Lily said, making it clear that she wasn't giving in on the subject. 'And then I am going to get a car.'

'Tell you what, when things are a bit more settled, I'll *buy* you a car. A belated wedding present,' he added, proceeding to kiss her rather more thoroughly now. But Lily felt as if she was being placated and she wriggled away 'Abigail will be here soon.'

'I promise I'll be quick.' He grinned that devilish grin, only this time she didn't smile back.

'What's wrong, Lily?' He must have sensed her disquiet, because he wasn't trying to kiss her now, his voice so tender, so concerned that for a second she forgot the rules.

'I hardly see you…' She could have bitten her

tongue off as the words spilled out, but Hunter just smiled.

'Hey, you're starting to sound like a *real* wife.'

'I'm just not used to it,' Lily said carefully, 'I'm used to being...' She flailed for the right word, struggled to retract the neediness that had crept into the conversation, to pull back from the line they had agreed not to cross. 'I suppose I'm used to working more, going out with friends, hopping into *my* car for a drive...'

'The summer holidays are over soon,' Hunter reminded her. 'You'll be able to find out about finishing that degree and we've got a big charity ball at the weekend to go to. Why don't you go and buy yourself something nice?'

He was trying to help, but he just didn't understand, could never understand, because she simply couldn't tell him—it wasn't her day or her wardrobe that needed filling, it was her mind. Though over and over Lily told herself to relax and enjoy it, to make the best of their time together, to go with the flow and enjoy the experience with every buff the manicurist applied to her nails, with every glittering bauble Hunter showered her with she felt as if her own sparkle was fading, as if somehow he was draining her, would take his fill till there was nothing left then discard the carcass. But instead of telling him that she nodded, said yes because it was easier than saying no, accepted his offer because it was safer than arguing, safer than revealing what was really in her heart.

'Right.' He squeezed her thigh through the sheet and glanced at his watch. 'Abigail will be...' His voice trailed off as he stood up, and she watched as the colour drained from his face, as he screwed his eyes closed and sat back down. With mounting alarm she watched as he buried his face in his hands.

'Hunter?' Appalled, Lily knelt, wrapped an arm around his shoulder, but by then it was over, Hunter shaking his head as if to clear it and even looking faintly embarrassed as he let out a long breath.

'Sorry about that.'

'Are you OK?' Her voice was urgent even

though the moment had passed—the colour in his face normal now, there was even a rueful smile on his lips. But she knew what she'd seen, knew that just a moment ago he'd been about to pass out. 'Hunter, you should lie down.'

'I'm fine.'

'No,' Lily argued, 'you're not. I'll ring Abigail and tell her you're taking the day off.'

'Lily.' He shrugged off concern, fixed her with a stare that told her to stay well back. 'Now you're really starting to scare me—you're actually starting to *act* like a real wife.' He flashed her a very on-off smile.

'I'm allowed to worry about you, Hunter,' Lily argued, refusing to back off, refusing to be silenced. 'You keep getting these headaches, your schedule's ridiculous. Sooner or later it has to catch up.'

'Worrying about me isn't in your job description,' Hunter broke in, slapping her back with harsh words.

'Oh, that's right.' Pulling the sheet around her, Lily headed for the bathroom, his words ricocheting through her, tears appallingly close. She was desperate to get away from him, to break down in private. 'I'm just the good-time girl—well, excuse me for forgetting.'

Sitting on the sofa, nursing a mug of coffee, still bristling from his words, Lily stared out at the view. The city was filling with morning traffic, tiny dots of people heading to work, to school. Part of her wished she were among them, wished she were down there, wrestling with the crowds, wished almost that she'd never met Hunter because that would mean she'd never have to miss him.

And she would miss him.

Biting on her lips to hold back tears, Lily tried to glimpse her future, tried to imagine a world without Hunter, but it was like driving with the windshield fogging up. Every thought of him that she attempted to wipe away came back thicker and faster, the road ahead almost impossible to envision without this impossible, difficult man in her life.

It was almost a relief when Abigail arrived.

Efficient as ever, Abigail stalked into the vast lounge and gave Lily the vaguest of nods as she turned her pussycat smile on Hunter, who was punching two headache tablets out of a blister pack.

'Morning, Hunter, you're looking a bit peaky.'

'Morning, Abigail, you're sounding a bit grating.'

At least his poisonous tongue wasn't solely reserved for her! Hugging her knees, Lily carried on staring out at the view, listening and not reacting as Abigail took him through his appalling schedule for the day—a TV interview in an hour, a board meeting at ten. She wondered how on earth anyone could cram it all on—how anyone could consider it normal.

'Are you sure you're OK?' Abigail checked again as Hunter picked up his briefcase. 'If you want I can arrange a doctor's appointment for you, we've got a bit of room for manoeuvre around 2 p.m.'

'Just a suggestion,' Abigail said as Hunter

swore under his breath. Clearly she was made of sterner stuff because, unlike Lily, she didn't fly off to the bathroom in tears, just laughed as they headed out of the door. 'If I didn't know better, I'd say you had a hangover.'

He didn't even bother to kiss her as he left and Lily couldn't even look up and say goodbye either. How long she sat there she wasn't sure—certainly long enough for Hunter to make it to the TV studios because, staring in recognition, she turned to the screen as his rich deep voice reached her ears, those dark eyes flirting with a million stay-at-home wives as he somehow put the sex into the ASX. Even the interviewer was blushing beneath her heavy foundation as she congratulated him on his recent nuptials!

'It *was* a very sudden wedding,' she said. 'Was there any reason for the haste?'

'I'm used to making snap decisions.' Hunter expertly deflected her. 'And as my track record shows, more often than not I'm right.'

'And yet, despite your success, your new wife

is *still* working…' she fished, but Hunter gave a seemingly bemused frown, managed, even if it was just for the audience, a dash of political correctness.

'Are you saying you have a problem with married women working?'

'Of course not,' the interviewer flustered, no doubt envisioning the rating figures dropping behind her frantic eyes. 'It's been suggested over the weekend that there might be some more good news forthcoming…' Her glossy smile was strained, waiting for Hunter to speak, to confirm or deny the pregnancy rumors, but he didn't even respond, forcing the interviewer to push harder. 'In the papers on Sunday you would have read—'

'I've only been married four weeks.' Hunter flashed a smile to the camera and surely melted every woman watching. 'As you've needlessly pointed out, my wife has chosen to continue with her career. Now, I'm sure you're viewers will understand if we have better things to do on our precious weekends than read the papers!'

'Of course,' she croaked, blushing furiously and shuffling the notes on her lap. 'I see that your own company's shares have increased by eight per cent since your marriage. Do you think investor confidence may be up—?'

'Eight point two,' Hunter interrupted. 'My company's shares are up by eight point two per cent. So clearly investors have every reason to feel confident.' There was a smile on his face, but his eyes had a warning glint in them, as if daring the interviewer to go on, challenging her to cross the line and delve into his private life further.

She didn't!

'Well, congratulations,' she offered again, 'on both counts.'

God, he was good! Even in her annoyance Lily couldn't fail to be impressed—that interviewer hadn't stood a chance. Still, the scrutiny unnerved Lily. It was OK for Hunter—he was used to having cameras trained on him, used to dealing with publicity and innuendo. Not only was she having to deal with the shock in the glossies that Hunter Myles had married a nobody, now they were suggesting…

Like a switch turning up the heat, the vague disquiet that till now had been bubbling unacknowledged seared into the boil of panic—the throw-away comment Hunter had made about her being pregnant jarring at her very core.

She couldn't be!

On shaky legs Lily headed for bag, pulled out her organiser and forced herself to face an issue she'd been desperately trying to avoid.

The exquisitely tender boobs, bursting into tears at the drop of a hat, almost fainting at Emma's recital…

She was on the Pill, for heaven's sake, Lily reassured herself as her manicured fingers flicked the pages. They'd only had unprotected sex once and she'd had her period almost straight afterwards.

Her fingers flicked over the pages, checking and checking again, her teeth working her bottom lip as she counted down the time since her last period…*six weeks ago!*

CHAPTER ELEVEN

'WERE you asleep?' Flicking on the light, Hunter sat on the edge of the bed as Lily lay there, trying to accustom her eyes to the light.

'Well, it is after one,' Lily said, peering at the bedside clock and deliberately yawning. He'd rung to say he was on his way home around nine, but by eleven, when even if there *had* been an accident, surely the police would have managed to inform her, she had taken herself and what she hoped was her overactive imagination to bed with a good book. After Hunter's harsh words that morning, she'd absolutely refused to play the part of the worried wife or aggrieved lover and ring to check where he was—and she was so glad she had. Hunter actually looked a bit put out as he undressed, but he didn't bother to climb into the bed, instead lying shamelessly on the top and, as was his usual style, completely oblivious to the ungodly hour, turning on a CD. Picking up her book, he started to skim-read a few pages. 'Do anything nice today?'

'Lots,' Lily answered brightly. 'I had a meeting at the centre—turned down the opportunity to start up a support group for teenagers recovering from eating disorders. In fact, I was the perfect little wife today. I took myself shopping and needlessly spent lots of your lovely money, then went and had a facial and pedicure. Oh, and I didn't worry about you a single bit.' Nothing could have been further from the truth! She'd spent the entire day drenched in her own anxiety, hanging around the chemist at the shopping centre like a sixteen-year-old boy attempting to purchase condoms, Hunter's warning about the ever-present paparazzi making her too paranoid to buy a simple pregnancy test. So instead the afternoon had been spent surfing the net, trying to find out the early symptoms of pregnancy, each site she visited either reassuring or confusing her till she given in and, as if she'd been visiting some torrid website, carefully deleted her user history, so Hunter wouldn't be able to see which websites she'd visited. The only money she'd spent today was on the fabulous book he was holding in his hands, but she wasn't going to tell him that!

'Oh, and I've seen a fabulous picture I'd like for the entrance hall,' Lily added.

'Good girl.' Hunter grinned at her facetiousness and squeezed her thigh through the sheet as he read on. 'Now you're getting the idea. Oh, and you need a new dress for the ball.'

'I've got a wardrobe of new dresses,' Lily pointed out. 'What's it in aid of?'

'Sorry?'

'The ball?'

His hands stopped halfway through turning a page.

'What charity is it?'

'Spinal injuries.' Hunter shrugged and carried on reading.

'Oh!' Lily stared over at him, waiting for him to elaborate. They'd been to so many events. More often than not Lily didn't know what she was dressing for till Hunter picked up his car keys or summoned his driver, but, given Emma's injuries, she'd at least have expected a touch more interest. 'Is Emma going?'

'Why would she?' Hunter glanced over, his voice suddenly scathing. 'As the token victim, she's got a bit more style than that.'

'I was just…' Her voice trailed off, her nose wrinkling in concentration as she remembered a half-forgotten conversation when they'd first met.

'Is this the big charity ball you were talking about when we first met the one you're organising?'

'I told you it was.'

'No, Hunter.' Lily shook her head. 'You didn't.'

'You didn't actually turn them down?' Hunter stared over at her bemused frown. 'The support group…'

'I said I'd think about it,' Lily answered tactfully.

'You don't have to defer to me…' Hunter turned his attention back to the book, seemingly nonchalant, but she knew how hard it was for him to say the words. 'If you think you should do it, go for it.'

'I will.'

'This is actually a good book,' Hunter commented without looking up, completely changing the subject. 'What happened to her?'

'Sorry?' Lily frowned, her mind trying to gather all the snippets of information he constantly blasted her with, trying to keep track of his endless threads of conversation and somehow piece them together.

'What happened to her? I can't make it out.'

Only then did she realise he was talking about the book, and she let out a tiny incredulous laugh 'You haven't read the beginning and you probably won't read the end…'

'So?'

'You can't just open up and demand to know

what's happened. You're supposed to read the whole thing—it's like walking in on the last five minutes of a film and asking for the entire plot!'

'And what's so wrong with that?' Hunter frowned. 'So are you going to tell me?'

'No.' Lily let out an irritated sigh. 'Because I actually don't know *what* happened to her. That's what I've been up half the night trying to find out.'

'So you've no idea!' He raised his eyebrows. 'You're up to page 242 and you still don't know!' He carried on reading, his curiosity piqued now, at least for a little while. Lily stared over at him. Even after a month his beauty still astonished her, his restless splendour as he lay beside her still drawing her in. But it wasn't just his looks or his touch that enthralled her, it was the man she hadn't yet met that really kept her captivated, the man that slowly, *painfully* slowly was being revealed to her: the flashes of just plain *niceness* that utterly disarmed her; the dry humour that could always foster a smile. And the gentler side, too, that occasionally she was privy to. Every now and then she was treated to a glimpse of what it could be like to be truly adored by a man like Hunter—and it made her yearn for more, yearn for the man she was sure was there behind the expensive suit and snobby derisive voice.

Every now and then there were moments as perfect as this.

'What?' Hunter asked, as he caught her staring.

'Nothing,' Lily answered, but the smile on her lips faded as she watched him, appalled as he turned to the ending and started to read.

'You can't do that!' She grabbed at his wrist but he started to laugh, holding the book up higher and somehow managing to keep her back and read at the same time. 'If you tell me what happened to her, if you even hint at the ending, then I'll never ever forgive you.' She was on her knees now, reaching for her book, and they were both laughing, really laughing as he teased her, laughing as, despite her attempt at protest, somehow she let him. But suddenly it all changed, the atmosphere charging in a very different direction as nakedness hit, the innocence of the moment deliciously gone as Hunter, on cue, rose to the occasion.

'Now look what you've done,' Hunter admonished, staring down at his splendid erection. 'You just can't leave me alone for even five minutes, Lily! There I was, trying to quietly read….'

'Keep reading, then,' Lily said, but there was a provocative note to her voice that Hunter registered, a small pregnant pause that spoke volumes—energy, arousal crackling between them so potently Lily could feel the tiny hairs on her arms rise to the static charge between them.

'Keep reading,' Lily said huskily again, delivering a velvet-wrapped order, watching the bob of his Adam's apple, a beat of hesitation before he picked up the book and seemingly resumed reading as Lily knelt beside him.

His face obscured by the book made her braver somehow, no knowing eyes on hers, nothing to distract from his magnificent splendour. A low rumble of excitement stirred in her groin as her tentative fingers reached out for him, his blatant want growing in her hands. Never had she wanted him more, bringing her hungry lips to taste him, the soft feel of his skin on her tongue a contrast to the strength beneath it, one hand in her hair guiding her to where he needed her most, inhaling the soapy clean smell of him she took him deeper, hearing his moans of pleasure, the thump of the book falling to the floor as fingers laced into her hair.

'Lily.' His voice was a husky kiss, his pleasure completely hers as he delivered his salty kiss, and when afterwards as he slid her up his body, dragged her up to join him, clung to her so intensely, so fiercely, it truly felt as if he would he never let her go.

CHAPTER TWELVE

NORMALLY Hunter was up before the birds, showered and ready to go before she had even surfaced, but on this Monday morning it was Lily dressed and fragrant, smiling as he leant back on the pillow and closed his eyes. 'How come you're up so early? I thought you weren't working till eleven?'

'I've got an interview at nine!' Lily beamed as his eyes snapped open, taking a sip of her coffee as Hunter sat up in the bed. 'I rang the university last week and they've squeezed in an appointment.'

'You didn't say anything.'

'Didn't I?' Lily gave a vague shrug—she probably hadn't. Even though Hunter had remained in Melbourne for the past week he'd still been inordinately busy, as had Lily, organising and adapting to her life and surroundings. Hunter's *bland* apartment was now weighted with texture and colour, scented candles burning into the evening, glorious silk cushions and vast vases of flowers delightfully breaking the structured ambiences. The fact she'd forgotten to mention a brief phone call was hardly a big deal—or so she'd thought! 'I'll make you a coffee while you have a shower.'

'No.'

'Tea, then,' Lily offered, turning to go, blindly missing his angry point but stopping in her tracks as Hunter's voice followed her down the hall.

'I meant no to the interview.'

'Excuse me?'

She was sure she must have misheard and still Lily gave him the benefit of the doubt, frowning as she turned her head.

'You're not going to the interview, Lily, you're not going to university. You're needed here.'

'For what?' Lily gave a shocked incredulous laugh. 'To preen myself for when you come home, to rattle around in shops and spend a fortune on clothes and furniture? To meet you for lunch when Abigail can slot me in? I'm not even having this discussion with you, Hunter— we agreed I'd do this course and that's exactly what I'm going to do.'

Almost gibbering with rage, Lily marched to the kitchen, half expecting him to follow her, picking up the paper again and pretending to read. Only when it was clear he wasn't coming, only when she heard the sound of the shower being turned on did Lily let out a long-held breath and try to fathom what was taking place.

Subtly at first—so subtly she'd hardly even noticed—he commandeered her time, thwarted every arrangement she made. A hastily arranged lunch date with her new husband reason enough to cancel a vague plan to catch up with friends, an impromptu trip invite to join him in Sydney reason enough for Lily not to spend a couple of days at her mother's, his opposition to her getting a car…and now this.

'Lily?'

She didn't look up, didn't acknowledge him at all as he joined her at the breakfast table, just carried on reading the paper as he helped himself to coffee and pastries.

'Lily, what I said before, I think you misunderstood.'

Her lips pursed as she carried on reading the paper, her legs tightly crossed, one foot swinging to a rhythm of its own, she pointedly refused to discuss it.

'When I said you couldn't go to university, what I meant was there's no need. Abigail's been looking into it for you. Apparently you can complete your course online.'

'Online?' Now she spoke, shot out the word with an incredulous laugh that was completely devoid of humour. Because there was nothing funny about this, nothing funny about it at all. Again Hunter was telling her to subscribe to what he considered best. An independent woman, Lily could see the bricks of her luxurious prison rising around her and she moved quickly to pull them down, to make this man realise that she made her own rules, made up her own mind.

'Hunter, what the hell is Abigail sorting out my schooling for? She's your PA, or diary planner, or what ever she wants to call herself. But she's not mine, and for the record I don't want to study online, I want to finish my degree properly.'

'We've been through this.' Hunter voice was incredibly measured, but she could hear the mounting impatience behind it, as if he were talking to some belligerent two-year-old who was defying him. 'You're Mrs Lily Myles now…'

'I'm still my own person,' Lily flared.

'Not for the next eleven months,' Hunter said and she glimpsed his power, the might, the drive that tossed boundaries aside and propelled him forward. But up to this point his undeniable force had never been aimed at her—at least, not in a negative way, and the tiny doubts she had chosen to ignore, the tiny negative questions she had pushed aside all swirled together into one black hole as Hunter told her in no uncertain terms what he expected from her. 'In eleven months you can do what you like, Lily, walk around in scruffy jeans with your fellow students, discussing the bloody meaning of life, take on every bleating charity case that comes knocking at your door, drive to your student bashes in some beaten-up old car, but for the next few months, you'll act accordingly!'

'According to what?' Lily demanded. 'Come on, Hunter, according to what? You want me to be happy, you want to know exactly what I'm thinking, you want to make love to me over and over…'

'So you're not happy in bed?'

'It's not the bedroom that's the problem,' Lily responded angrily. Exasperation raising her voice, she jabbed a desperate finger at his chest then pointed it over and over to his head. 'It's here, Hunter. You want absolutely everything of me. You want me to be a *real* wife, to be with you, to tell you what I'm thinking, what I'm feeling, yet you give absolutely nothing back!'

'Do you want me to dig out the house deeds?'

Hunter's voice was pure ice. '*Nothing* is what you had when I met you!'

'You don't own me,' Lily flared, instinctively fighting back, refusing to be intimidated, stunned at the way he was behaving, sure that her anger, her fury would provoke a retraction from him. But instead she got a reaction, and one she had subconsciously been dreading—eyes, darkening in rage, lips that had always, to her at least, been kind curling in contempt as he spat out the words.

'Oh, but, I do. And don't you forget it.'

She felt as if she'd been hit, the sting of his words, the brutality of them hitting her with full force, momentarily stunning her. But she recovered quickly. Defiant, enraged, she faced him head on, absolutely refused to be intimidated by him.

'Never!' Just one word, one single word, but it was said with such strength, such conviction that it hit its mark, allowing her to glimpse just a flicker of doubt in his cool blue eyes, the tiniest of chinks in his impressive armour as her unwavering certainty reached him. It gave her the momentum to continue. 'And don't you ever, *ever* talk to me like that again, Hunter.' Her lips were numb with tension, but her voice was clear. 'Let's get things straight. I *am* going to carry on working, I *am* going to university, I *am* going to get a car, and if you *ever* talk to me like that again, I'll be out that door.'

On cue it opened. Abigail, crisp and elegant in a black suit, walked in and, no doubt sensing the tension, gave them both a wide smile.

'Crisis!'

'We're fine,' Lily snarled, but Abigail laughed.

'Glad to hear it, but I was actually talking about work!' Lily balled her hands into fists, more furious with herself for giving Abigail even a hint there was a problem. 'I'm afraid you're needed in Singapore.'

'When?' Hunter's voice was even, but his body was still taut with tension. The row was nowhere near over, there were so many unsaid words still sizzling between them as they both attempted to pretend everything was normal.

'We're on the 10 a.m. flight!'

* * *

There was nothing worse than an unfinished row.

Abigail had packed for him because, as Abigail had explained sweetly, she knew what Hunter needed, leaving Lily standing bristling in the lounge with him. Every now and then one of them would open their mouth to speak, then clearly think better of it, mindful there was nothing that could be said without revealing to Abigail's undoubtedly pricked ears the reason for their marriage.

It was Hunter who finally broke the strained silence.

'Will you be OK?' He sounded tired, as if all the fight had gone out of him, and Lily was appallingly close to crying, but she didn't let him see that. Better he think her a cold-hearted bitch than just another woman who adored him.

Loved him even?

'I'm sure I'll cope without you, Hunter.' She flashed her green eyes at him, directed at him the anger that was turned in on herself. 'It might take a while to work out my schedule or sort out my clothes in the morning without you doing it for me, but I'm sure I can muddle through till you get back.'

'Lily, don't.' His normally assured voice sounded weary with wretchedness so she toned it down a touch, even managed to feel sorry for him—a long flight and no doubt a frantic work day lay ahead, which made it a very long time till the sun set on this row. 'We'll talk when I get back, OK?'

Abigail appeared with her pussycat smile, wheeling Hunter's suitcase. 'All set?'

'Yep.' Hunter nodded and made to go then changed his mind, 'Actually, Abigail, I'll meet you down at the car.'

'If we're going to catch that flight, Hunter, we really need to move now.'

'I said,' Hunter growled, 'that I'd meet you down at the car. Now, can I have five bloody minutes' peace with my wife?'

Lily's only solace in the whole wretched morning was the indignant look on Abigail's face as she very reluctantly took herself out of the door.

'It's like putting out the cat in a storm,' Hunter said once the door was safely closed. It was such an apt description that despite her misery Lily managed a wobbly smile. 'I'm actually going to ask her for the key today—she can use the intercom, like everyone else.'

'Can't have her barging in on us rowing.' Lily offered a feeble joke, still shaking from the argument and all it had unleashed.

He dragged a hand through his hair, and for once it didn't fall back perfectly. For once he didn't look like the Hunter she'd first met. Exhaustion seeped from him, those stunning, direct eyes now puzzled and weary.

That was exactly how he felt.

There she stood, confused, wary, defiant and so incredibly beautiful, so, so...*vulnerable*.

He loathed the way he was acting, loathed the vile tirades that came out of his mouth, loathed that he had reduced them to this. All the fun, all the heady excitement that had brought them together dissipated further with every outburst, but it *had* to be this way, Hunter reminded himself. With every night they spent together, with every shared laugh, shared kiss he could feel them blending, two separate ingredients forming one so sweet, so infinitely desirable it was torturous not to sample, but if ever self-control was called for it was now.

He wanted to keep her safe—safe from the future he might provide.

Reaching out, expecting her to flinch, to push his hand away, relief suffused him as his hand captured her cheek, as she rested her head into palm, her soft skin beneath his fingers, her delicate fragrance reaching him.

'What's wrong, Hunter?'

'Nothing.' He closed his eyes as he answered, her question so genuine, her voice so tender it was impossible to look into her eyes and lie.

'Something is,' she insisted gently. 'And if I can help…'

'You can't.' His voice came out way too harsh, yet still he could feel her warmth, feel the infinite well of her caring, and it terrified him. He wanted to tell her so much, he actually wanted to lean on her, to have *her* hold *him.*

'Is it Emma?' It was as if she was mirroring his soul. 'Your parents?'

'I'm fine.'

'These headaches you're getting—'

'They're nothing.'

'Are you drinking?' Snapping his eyes open, the direct question so far from the answer it brought an incredulous smile to his lips.

'Where the hell did you pluck that from? You *know* I don't drink.'

'I don't *know* anything about you.' Her voice was still soft, her eyes two deep pools of concern. 'I just see these moods, the headaches, the *pain* you seem to be in. If there is something going on, maybe you can tell me. Maybe I can help…'

Oh, God, he wanted to tell her, wanted to tell her what was worrying him, what drove him over and over to push her away. Momentarily he faltered, his mouth opening to speak, to vomit out the pain that was churning in his soul. But she must have sensed his weakness, sensed his desire to tell, because as she confirmed he could go on, that soft voice telling him that *maybe she could help him*, as surely as if she'd slapped him, Hunter pulled back.

The sound of his father's stick banging on the bedroom floor, beating in time to the throb of his neuralgia, as she blindly offered to stand by him. And it wasn't an idle promise— Hunter knew that.

He knew, with a certainty that chilled him to the marrow, she meant it.

He had to protect her from himself at *all* costs.

'Look, I've got to go.'

'We need to talk.'

'We will when I get back,' Hunter simultaneously lied as he promised. 'I'll be gone three, maybe four days. I have to be back for the ball on Saturday.' He gave a tiny wince. 'It's your birthday on Saturday, too…'

'It's no big deal.'

'I'll make sure I'm back by Friday. You're sure you'll be OK?'

'It's not your job to worry.' Lily said it without malice, just affirmed the wretched rules they had agreed to. She expected a wry smile or even a *'Touché,'* but she was stunned when he shook his head.

'It's not that easy, though, is it?'

And despite the row, despite the vile start to the day, it was the closest they'd ever been, the closest he'd ever come to acknowledging *them,* and at that moment she couldn't pretend, couldn't let him get on a plane without saying a little of what was in her heart.

'No, it isn't that easy,' she admitted slowly. 'Maybe if I was your glamorous mistress and we saw each other once a week for fabulous no-strings sex then we could play by the rules. But living together, lo—' She choked back the word and quickly rephrased it. '*Laughing* together, sharing our families, it's impossible not to care.' He gave a tired nod of understanding and it gave her the courage to continue. 'I *am* worried about you. Please, tell me what's going on.'

'There's *nothing* going on.' The tiny whirlwinds that danced on their horizon blackened then, an updated forecast looming in Lily's mind, and suddenly she was scared for him, knew for certain that he was lying.

'I don't believe you,' Lily said softly.

'It's really nothing,' he said more firmly, though it was almost as if he was trying to convince himself rather than her. 'I'm just tired, I guess. Can't stand the thought of getting on another plane, crashing out in another hotel.'

'Do you have to go today?'

'Yes.'

'And so do I,' Lily said. All the anger gone from them now and he actually nodded his understanding. 'This is something I have to do.'

An impatient buzz on the intercom, no doubt from Abigail, fractured the rare moment of true intimacy, and Hunter reluctantly withdrew and gave her the briefest but most tender of kisses before picking up his briefcase and heading for the door.

'Hey, Lily.' He turned and smiled, looking far more like the usual Hunter and certainly sounding it when he spoke. 'When all this is over, do you think we might manage that?'

'Manage what?'

'You as my glamorous mistress and meeting once a week for fabulous sex? I mean, I know we said we'd just end it, but…'

'Worried you might miss me?' Lily raised a teasing eyebrow, even managed an easy wave as he headed out of the door, but her heart was hammering in her chest. She was almost relieved when he had gone so that she could let out the breath she was holding, could sit down on the couch and gather the thoughts that were swirling in her mind like a snowstorm.

They'd agreed to walk away at the end of a year, agreed to stay out of each other's lives, and, whether joking or not, Hunter had given her a glimpse that he wasn't finding things particularly easy either.

It was as if the ground had suddenly shifted—the rules that had been rigidly set melting like ice cubes on a warm day—only it wasn't just Lily who was flouting them.

CHAPTER THIRTEEN

'CONGRATULATIONS, Lily!'

Lily shook the hand of her much-admired professor as the interview concluded, the smile on her face so wide as she left his office she was almost tempted to burst into giggles as she headed for Administration.

She was back—back to a place where life had been wonderful. A time before her father had died, a time before those wretched letters had blown apart her world, back to a place where she belonged.

And it was thanks to Hunter.

However much he'd opposed it that morning, Lily thought as she filled out the endless forms that were required, it had been Hunter who had suggested it, Hunter who had made it possible,

Hunter who had made her delve deep and admit to her innermost dream, and for that she'd always be grateful.

'The banking forms are missing.' Lily handed over the wad of forms to a rather harassed receptionist. 'I'd like to pay in monthly installments, please.'

'It's all been taken care of.' Printing off a sheet, she handed it to Lily. 'Your husband's assistant rang through this morning. Sorry.' She reached out for a ringing telephone. 'I need to get this.'

He'd paid.

Lily's eyes welled with tears as she read the form, saw that he'd paid in full for her tuition, had even provided credit for books. It wasn't the money that moved her—it was the thought behind it. Jewellery, a car, a house—nothing could compare to this. Education, to Lily, was the greatest gift, increasing her knowledge so she could reach out to others—those that wanted to be reached, anyway.

* * *

'It's just one or two to unwind in the evening.' Dishevelled, anxious, Jinty gave the group an attempt at a smile. The whole, exhausting session—in fact, the last few weeks both in group and individually—had been heavily focused on Jinty's recent return to drinking, and though optimistic for her client's sake, even Lily was starting to wonder if she'd ever break through the fog of denial engulfing Jinty. 'I know what you're all thinking, but it's nothing like that.'

'Nothing like what, Jinty?' Lily asked, listening to the resounding silence, broken only by a couple of coughs from the group before finally Jinty answered.

'Nothing like before.'

Before, when her life had fallen apart—before, when she'd absolutely refused to face up to the world and its problems. Sadly, if Jinty didn't want to see it, chose not to face it, there was absolutely nothing Lily could do except listen and hopefully, when she was ready, still be there for her.

'It's all right for you.' Jinty suddenly snarled her rage focused directly at Lily, her anger palpable.

But far from being shocked, Lily welcomed it with relief. 'You sit there in your posh dress, with your fancy driver outside, and tell us where we're all going wrong. You don't have to worry about bills and kids and an ex...' On and on she went, tears, loathing choking every word, until finally it was over, her denial parting for a second, just long enough to choke the words they'd all been waiting to hear, absolute terror in her voice as she stilled just long enough to see her past and glimpse a futile future.

'I don't want to go back there.'

Lachlan was waiting for her in the car park, quickly stubbing out a cigarette and rushing round to open the door as, drooping with mental exhaustion, Lily walked over. She waved for him to relax.

'I'm going to do some shopping, take a walk perhaps.'

'That's fine. Would you like me to wait here, Mrs Myles, or—?'

'Thanks, Lachlan, but I won't be needing you

today,' Lily broke in, brave all of a sudden and knowing what she had to do. Her troubled clients had unwittingly given back just as much insight as they'd received. If Jinty could face her fears then surely so could she. 'I'll be making my own way home.'

'Congratulations, *Mrs Brown*!' For the second time that day Lily accepted the congratulations graciously, shook another doctor's hand, then headed to Reception and paid in cash for her consultation. Only the similarities didn't end there. Heading out onto the busy city street, watching the world carrying on as normal as her entire world shifted, Lily found she was smiling, *really* smiling. The news she had dreaded, the utter panic that had filled her whenever she had dared to think about this moment curiously absent, the impossibility of the future put on hold for just a little while as she focused on the present—she was definitely having a baby. Hunter's baby. And even if it was the last thing she'd planned, the last thing she'd wanted to happen, she didn't feel cheated or trapped. Whatever Hunter's reaction, Lily knew in her heart that she'd manage, that both she and the little life inside her would be OK.

Staring up at the sky, watching the silver speck of a jet plane winging its way to a destination unknown, the smile faded from her lips, a shiver of fear running through her.

Hunter couldn't go on like this and it was starting to show. The endless, merciless schedule, the constant sex. It was like watching a beautiful tapestry being slowly but surely unpicked—black moods that seemed to come from nowhere, the sheer exhaustion that at times literally seeped from him.

She and the baby would be OK. Lily knew she could deal with it, that she wasn't the first or last woman to deal with an unplanned pregnancy, that she had enough love within her to share.

No, it wasn't the baby or herself that she was scared for—it was Hunter.

CHAPTER FOURTEEN

'YOU look fabulous!' Smiling up at her in the doorway, Emma would normally have been the most welcome of visitors. Normally Lily would have been thrilled to have Emma drop by.

Only there was nothing normal about this evening—not that she told Emma that!

'I'm not breaking anything up, I hope?' Emma checked, her eyes anxiously darting to the beautifully laid table, sniffing the lamb that was roasting in the oven. 'Stupid me—you two haven't seen each other in days! I'll go...'

'Don't be daft.' Lily smiled. 'And, no, you're not breaking up anything. Hunter's still not back. He rang and said he was having trouble at customs.'

'But he cleared customs hours ago. I rang him

and he…' Her voice trailed off, perhaps registering Lily's bemused expression, and quickly reassured her. 'I must have misheard him he must have been just *about* to go through!'

'Probably.' Lily shrugged, trying to inject some lightness into her voice as Emma pushed her chair along the polished floorboards. 'Or he might just have stopped off at the office on his way home and forgotten the time.'

'Well, he's an idiot, then,' Emma said stoutly. 'Because you look stunning!'

Lily had actually felt *fabulous* and *stunning* a few hours ago. Not so guiltily she'd purchased the softest, blackest, most divine cashmere dress, which sat just above the knee and clung to her body like a second skin, perhaps a rather warm second skin for a hot summer night, but that was the beauty of Hunter's apartment—the temperature could be controlled with flick of a switch.

Unlike Hunter, Lily thought darkly.

Where the hell was he?

It had been five days and four extremely long

nights since he'd left for Singapore, since he'd promised they'd actually talk. Over and over Lily had wondered what he'd have to say, while attempting to fathom how to tell him her own huge news!

'I just wanted to check that he was OK.' Emma pulled herself out of the wheelchair and sank into the suede sofa, smiling gratefully as Lily put it away out of sight. It had become if not a routine then an unspoken ritual that had evolved whenever Emma came around to visit, as if somehow with the beastly chair out of sight, Emma could forget its existence for a moment, sit on the sofa in her brother's apartment and gossip with his new wife, forget for a moment the restraints. And in its own way the absence of the chair helped Lily, too—allowed her perhaps to forget one of the real reasons she was there. Parking the chair, Lily made her way back to join Emma on the sofa as she resumed the conversation. 'I wasn't sure how he'd be, what with today being our parents' anniversary and everything. Especially with him being in

Singapore.' Thankfully, Lily was just about to sit. Her back was to Emma's so she didn't see the shock on her face as the importance of the day was revealed—a detail that surely a *real* wife would know.

'It must be hard for him, being away from everyone…' Lily took a sip of water, her mouth impossibly dry as she swallowed down the latest update on what was happening in her husband's life. 'But apart from a quick call from the airport before he took off, I haven't really spoken to him. I really don't know how he's doing.'

'I've been looking at my watch all day. You know the sort of thing—thinking that this time last year I was walking. In fact, at this very moment I was in Singapore, too, chatting to Mum, Dad and Hunter, putting on my make-up and waiting to go on stage.'

'In Singapore?' Emma was too wrapped up in her own grief to hear the confusion in Lily's voice, shards of information stabbing her, glimpses of realisation starting to hit.

'The stupid thing is, had it been any other night I'd have caught a taxi with a few friends and we'd have gone somewhere cheap and cheerful to eat.' Emma closed her eyes in bitter regret, taking a moment to regroup before continuing. 'You know, no matter how many times I go over that night, I know it's only a fraction of the amount Hunter must do it. He blames himself.' Lily felt her heart still in her chest as Emma spoke, felt fingers of fear clutch at her heart at the certainty in Emma's voice as she spoke on. 'This ball we're going to tomorrow…'

'I thought you weren't going.'

'I am now.' Emma gave a tight shrug. 'Hunter's never done a thing for charity and suddenly he's organising a ball in aid of spinal injury research—'

'Research?' Lily checked, voicing the word Hunter had omitted.

'He thinks he can somehow fix this.' Emma gave a wan smile. 'He thinks somehow he can make up for what happened. He can deny it all he likes but I know it's eating him up.'

'But it wasn't his fault!' Lily croaked, trying to find out more without revealing just how little she knew. 'I mean, it's not as if he was driving—it was an accident.'

'Thank God you're here to keep telling him that.' Emma smiled her engaging smile. 'Till you came along, he was on a collision course for disaster. He simply won't talk about it with me, just buries himself in his ridiculous schedules and even more ridiculous social life. I know he's still working at a frenetic pace, but at least he's got you to come home to, you to confide in now.'

Only he didn't confide.

Every time she'd broached this sensitive topic, Hunter had either turned up the music or turned on the charm, thus avoiding the issue.

And it was an issue.

She knew that now.

It was Lily looking at the clock now, wishing she could see him, talk to him, wishing he would let her be there for him—wishing she knew what the hell had happened that night.

'I still can't believe it, actually!'

'Believe what?' Lily asked, forcing her mind away from Hunter and back to Emma.

'That not only is my eternally single brother married, but I actually *like* who he's with!'

'I bet you say that to all the girls.' Lily gave a wry smile, could hear the jealousy in her words no matter how she tried to keep her voice light.

'Oh, Hunter's had plenty of girlfriends, that's for sure.' Emma laughed, but, sensing perhaps she'd touched a nerve, her laughter faded. 'He married you though, Lily, and don't ever forget it. You just have to look at the two of you together to see how much you adore each other.'

And Emma must have been as lousy a judge of character as her own mother was, Lily thought, because her attempt at comfort was genuine—Emma truly believed that Hunter had married her for nothing other than love. 'Can I tell you something, Lily, between us?'

'*Just* between us?' Lily checked nervously.

'I'd rather you didn't say anything to Hunter.' Emma gave a tight shrug. 'Look, I know that's perhaps a bit unfair, to ask you to keep something from him, but I hope we're more than just *relatives*. I hope that we're friends, too.'

Oh, God, she'd never envisaged this. Not for a second, when she'd agreed to the marriage, had she considered that she might actually like Hunter's family. She adored Emma, and if it had been a real marriage, if Emma was actually her *real* sister-in-law about to spill her secrets, about to invite her right into her world, Lily would have embraced it. Instead, she recoiled. Instead of leaning forward, she muttered something about getting a drink and stood up, headed to the kitchen and opened some freshly prepared dips from the restaurant below, poured perfectly chilled wine into a slender glass for her guest, praying that Emma would have regrouped, that the moment of closeness, of friendship and trust would have passed.

It hadn't.

'You know how I've been seeing Jim an awful lot, and, Lily…' Her voice was brimming with excitement. 'I think that this is it.'

'It?'

'That he's the one.' Emma gave a tiny shocked giggle. 'I can't believe I'm even thinking it, let alone admitting to anyone. He's amazing. For the first time in my life I feel as if someone loves me just for me, and I'm not just talking about since the accident. I've never felt like this before. I've never met someone I could so completely open up to, love so unashamedly…' She looked over at Lily, clearly expecting some sort of affirmation and bemused when none was forthcoming.

'You don't seem very pleased.'

'Of course I'm pleased, it's just…' Lily raked her fingers through her hair as she worked out what to say. 'Emma, you've only known him a month.'

'You'd only known Hunter two weeks before you were married.' Emma laughed. 'If anyone should understand a whirlwind relationship, Lily, it should be you!'

Lily was saved from a response by Hunter's incredibly delayed arrival—and her eyes narrowed in concern as he walked in, his complexion grey, his stance utterly exhausted but still with enough dash about him to fill the room.

'Hi, honey.' Drooping with weariness, he planted a kiss, and it churned Lily's stomach as it landed on Emma's cheek rather than hers, the tender reunion she'd been secretly hoping for dissipating further if that were possible. 'I didn't know you were coming over—customs was a bloody nightmare.'

'Poor you,' Emma groaned in sympathy. 'Never mind, I've been keeping your lovely new wife company—someone has to. Oh, hi, Abigail!' she added as the woman herself breezed in the door, looking more like she'd stepped out of a beauty parlor than a plane. Her hair and make-up were immaculate, her suit completely unruffled, and she raised a perfectly tweezed eyebrow as she surveyed first the room and then Lily, the tiniest hint of a smirk on her face as she zipped open her bag and pulled out a small silver laptop.

'Do you want me to check if those figures are

in, Hunter? Then I can prepare the report for your morning meeting.'

'Please.' Hunter yawned without covering his mouth, then planted a rather haphazard kiss on Lily's cheek, barely even glancing in her direction—the hours of preparation she'd put in for this moment, the thrill of anticipation at their reunion dissipating as Hunter practically ignored her, chatting amicably with Emma, with his back half turned to her. Feeling like an outsider in her temporary home, Lily stood up and retreated to the kitchen, but there was no solace to be found there. Abigail had beaten her to it, frothing the milk like some professional barista, rescuing the burnt lamb Lily had lovingly prepared from the oven and slicing it onto bread.

'You don't mind?' Abigail checked with a sweet smile that was definitely false. 'Only Hunter's starving.'

'Help yourself,' Lily retorted, refusing to jump to the bait, refusing to belittle herself as her lovingly prepared dinner was shredded before her eyes but allowing herself the luxury of pointing out an obvious fact. 'After an evening spent in customs, he probably wants to just eat and go to bed.'

'Customs?' Abigail turned and crinkled her pretty nose, her botoxed forehead attempting to frown and spectacularly failing! 'I've no idea what you're talking about. We cleared customs in five minutes.'

'I thought they'd never go!' Hunter rolled his eyes as he finally closed the door on their un-invited guests. And now that they were alone, now there was nothing to distract him, he graced her with his attention, pulling her into his arms and burying his face in her neck, holding her fiercely against him, just as she had imagined he would—only several hours and a whole lot of hurt too late. 'God, I'm ex-hausted, Lily.' He almost groaned the words out, his hungry mouth for once not searching for hers, just holding her against him, almost leaning on her. Screwing her eyes closed, she fought resistance, knew that no matter how much he denied it today was a brutal day for him, knew that even if he couldn't admit it, today he was hurting like hell—and it would be so easy to put her feelings on hold for tonight, so, so easy to ignore the questions that were buzzing in her mind and give him the comfort he craved. But she knew there and then she couldn't do it for a second longer.

Couldn't make love to him without revealing how she felt; couldn't give just her body for even one more night.

Couldn't be the wife he wanted.

'I need to clear up.' Ducking her head, she tried to pull back, but Hunter held her tight.

'The cleaner will be here in the morning,' he murmured. 'Let's got to bed—I've got to be up at six.'

But she wriggled out of his arms and proceeded to clear away the glasses and plates that littered the table.

'Leave it, Lily.'

Ignoring him, Lily carried the dishes through, staring at the remains of the dinner she had so carefully prepared hacked to pieces by Abigail as Hunter followed her in.

'Can we just go to bed?'

'You don't need my permission to go to bed, Hunter.' Lily filled the sink and flicked on the tap. 'You go in and I'll be in when I'm ready.'

'I'm sorry I was late and ruined the dinner.' His voice was tense, each word bristled out through strained lips. 'I'm sorry that Emma and Abigail stayed so long, but I've had one hell of a day and right now I just want to go to bed—with my wife!'

He was practically shouting, his voice rising with each word, and any hope Lily had of avoiding confrontation tonight faded. Her eyes were equally livid when she turned to face him, furious that he thought a burnt dinner was all she was upset about—that he could really think she was *that* stupid.

'Where were you this afternoon?'

'What?'

'You heard.' Lily didn't even blink as he spat out his answer with a question.

'What is this?' He shook his head and gave an incredulous snort. It enraged her—that he so clearly thought she didn't even have the right to ask, that he dared to think she would just meekly follow him to bed without knowing where the hell he'd been.

'Your plane got in at three and you told Emma you'd cleared customs.'

'So?' He turned his back on her and went to walk off, and if there was one thing Lily was good at, if there was one thing her time studying psychology at university had taught her, it was that when dealing with an evasive person, to form watertight arguments, to stick to the point and deal with facts. And Hunter was being supremely evasive, trying to change the subject, answering each straightforward question with an accusation of his own and, Lily realised with a sinking heart, lying to her. 'You then walked through the door and said that customs had been hell, yet Abigail said in the kitchen that you'd cleared customs in five minutes.'

'Where's the transcript?' Hunter sneered, 'I

wasn't aware you were taking notes of every-thing I said.'

'Where were you, Hunter?'

'Paying for your new dress,' Hunter roared. 'Paying for your house and the interior designer to come and fix this apartment to your tastes. Did it never enter your head I might have to go to the office?'

'I rang the office.' Tears sparkled in her eyes but she blinked them back, her voice hoarse with emotion but somehow strong. 'You weren't there, so—'

'So you assumed I was in bed with Abigail, assumed that if I wasn't on the end of the line, waiting to pick up your call, I must be out screwing.'

'Where were you, Hunter?' It was the third time she'd asked the question, but practice didn't make it any easier. Each evasive answer he gave twisted the knife in her heart further. She was scarcely able to comprehend that just a few hours ago she'd been planning to tell him about the pregnancy over a beautiful home-cooked meal, to reveal that, actually, she loved him, that right up until a few moment ago somehow, despite the odds, she'd always trusted him.

'Why bother asking when you've already made up your mind?' His blue eyes stared at her coolly.

'You said that you'd be faithful.'

'And you said you'd be fun!' He shrugged his shoulders at her shocked gasp, the anger gone from his voice now. She almost wished it back because anything was better than the icy disdain, his complete dismissal. 'I guess neither of us really knew what we were letting ourselves in for.'

'You bastard!'

'Apparently so.'

He turned to go then changed his mind, anger back in his eyes as her faced her.

'Did it never enter your head that there might be a reason *other* than that I was sleeping with Abigail? Did you never think that today's my parents' anniversary, that perhaps I was upset and went to the cemetery?'

Guilt tripped it's switch, but didn't dim her hurt—the impossibility of living with him, of only being privy to the tiniest part of him taking its toll now. Her voice was thick with emotion when finally she answered him. 'How, Hunter?' she rasped. 'How could it have entered my head when I didn't even know it was their anniversary? How could I have possibly even thought it when you didn't even tell me the accident happened in Singapore? Where you were today? You tell me absolutely nothing about how you're feeling or thinking or what's happening…'

'I've just told you where I was. I've just told you how I felt.'

'But look what the hell we had to go through to get there!' She was crying now, hot choking tears streaming down her face as she tried to face this impossible man. 'I don't think I can do this any more, Hunter. I don't think I can carry on like this. I can't keep giving myself and getting nothing back.' And though it was a plea for help, for understanding, for them to somehow sit down and rewrite the rules they had drawn up, it was also a confrontation, because surely if he felt anything for her on an emotional level, now was the time to reveal it. Surely if he did want a new level of intimacy then now was the time to tell her, show her. 'I don't know if I can keep sharing your bed, keep—'

'Then do us both a favour and don't!' He broke into her heartfelt attempt to explain with such a curt, dismissive tone, such brutal detachment it more than served than its purpose. The river of tears dried up instantly as her shocked mind absorbed his words. 'You know, I think twelve months was stretching it—even twelve weeks is looking untenable.'

'So that's it?' Lily whispered.

'Pretty much.' Hunter gave a dismissive shrug. 'Emma seems happier, my investors are grinning…' He shot her a black grin of his own. 'You've more than served your purpose!'

She'd almost told him she loved him. Lily could scarcely believe that just a few seconds ago even in the midst of an angry row she'd been prepared to take that gamble, to expose that last piece of herself to him. But with a few callous words he'd changed everything—his atrocious, immutable indifference, his appalling cruelty told her everything she didn't want to know.

She didn't say anything, didn't offer a response or a reaction as he shrugged his shoulders and headed for bed. The cold shock he'd plunged her into was curiously comforting, extricating emotion, enabling her to face the unpalatable truth.

Nothing was worth the pain he invariably inflicted—love not quite dazzling enough to blind her to the savagery of his words at times or the black moods that came from nowhere.

Numb, she picked up the mug he had been drinking from and sniffed at it, then, scarcely able to believe what she was doing, she rummaged through the kitchen cupboards, looking for what she didn't really know— alcohol, drugs, something, *anything* that might explain his behaviour. She even resorted to looking through his jacket pockets for evidence and then stopping. She couldn't go on like this—not just for her sake, but for the baby's, too.

She couldn't keep searching for an answer to a man who insisted there wasn't a problem.

Like a sleepwalker she headed for the couch and pulled down a throw rug. Huddling up, she stared out into the darkness, her hand on her stomach, acknowledging somehow the little life within.

Knowing it was up to her to protect it.

CHAPTER FIFTEEN

'HAPPY birthday!' After last night it should have been completely inappropriate, but it was delivered in such an ironic tone that when Hunter sighed and sat heavily on the couch beside where she'd slept, even Lily managed the palest of smiles. 'Abigail's going to accuse me of having a hangover again.' He massaged his temples, his blue eyes closed against the rising sun as he offered his apology—again.

'I'm sorry.' He dragged in some air though lips that were a touch too pale and finally opened his eyes and looked at her. 'I can't actually remember all I said last night, but I think even *I* excelled myself.'

'You did,' Lily gulped, unable to look back at

him, scared that she might forgive him and terrified that still she loved him.

'Last night when you said you couldn't go on...'

'I meant it,' Lily broke in quickly, scared she'd relent, that she'd somehow forget the pain of last night with the dawn of a new day. 'Hunter, I can't do this any more.'

'I know you can't.' He took her hand in his, and she knew she should pull back, knew she shouldn't let him in even a little bit, but somehow it was easier to hold onto him as she summoned the strength to leave him. 'And I can't either, Lily.'

'So that's it, then.' Lily sniffed, somehow managing not to crumble, willing herself to get through the next little bit without tears before she cried a river alone. 'Look, I know we have to talk,' she said to herself more than to him, trying to draw a wobbly map to see her through the blur of the immediate future. 'I know we're going to have to sort out what we're going to tell everyone, that sort of thing, but can it wait a couple of days? I'll be out of here by the time you get back.'

'No.' It was Hunter shaking his head now, Hunter's hand holding hers. 'After last night I can fully understand that you want to leave, that you want this to end, but, *please,* can we do the talking first? I know I'm lousy at saying how I feel, but maybe—'

'No!' Lily snapped the word out and managed now to look at him. 'I can't keep on doing this, Hunter,' she repeated, just so he got it, just so he knew there was no room for any more hurt. 'I believe you went to the cemetery, but for four hours?' She shook her head at the impossibility of it. 'And with Abigail?'

'OK.' He screwed his eyes closed as she confronted him. 'I wasn't just at the cemetery.'

'Then where?'

'Look, yesterday was a bad day for me, Lily. A *really* bad day,' he offered as if by upping the explanation he could excuse his actions. 'And I know I've hurt you, I know I haven't been upfront with you, but I promise you there's nothing between me and Abigail.'

'Which lie am I supposed to believe?' Lily

frowned. 'The one that fits best—the one that makes things more palatable—'

'We need to talk,' Hunter broke in. 'We both need to be honest.'

'But I've been honest,' Lily flared, but it quickly ebbed. Her lies by omission surely counted, too, and she lay back on the cushion, gave Hunter a window of opportunity to continue.

'I want you to keep being honest.' He was squeezing her hand so tightly it was starting to hurt. 'I want you to wait till we've spoken before you leave. Abigail will be here in a few minutes—I *have* to go and sort out things for the ball tonight. I have to see this through.' His eyes pleaded for understanding. 'Please, come to the ball, Lily. There's so much riding on tonight, I just can't let everyone down. Please, come and stand by my side, then we'll talk.'

'I don't know…' She shook her head help-lessly, scared of staying but terrified of leaving, too, watching as he reached into his jacket he pulled out a rather impressive silver envelope which she hesitantly opened.

'Tell Abigail, thanks.' If she was being churlish she didn't care. Being pampered in a day spa was the absolute last thing she wanted right now, especially if Abigail had ordered it and arranged it as usual.

'I booked it myself two days ago from Singapore.' Hunter dragged in a deep breath. 'Please, say that you'll come with me tonight.'

She didn't answer him because she truly didn't know what her answer was. She was just grateful for his shard of sensitivity that when Abigail, no doubt indignantly, buzzed on the intercom, instead of pressing for her to come in, Hunter picked up his briefcase to meet her halfway as Lily lay there, wondering whether or not she could do the same for Hunter.

However thoughtful Hunter's gift, it wasn't the best choice for a pregnant woman in a state of high anxiety. Especially one who hadn't yet told her husband! Paranoid, she ticked the 'no' boxes on the required forms but, reading the treatments on offer and the little information boxes beside them, Lily realised there was actually very little she could have.

The sauna was out, as were certain aromatherapy oils, deep-tissue massage. The list of what she couldn't have was endless so, settling for a spray-on tan, followed by a facial and having her hair styled, Lily tried hard to relax, tried to let her mind wander as skilled hands supposedly massaged away the tension. But no matter how far she drifted, it was as if there was an elastic band strapped to her waist, snapping her back to the present, to the issues, to the very reason she was there…

She'd accepted his gift and it truly terrified her. She could almost hear his silken voice as it delivered lies that maybe deep down she wanted to hear. She wondered if she'd be strong enough to adhere to the one boundary she had set, the one thing she'd asked of him. She didn't want to end up like her mother, eternally turning a blind eye in order to keep him, to give their child a father…Lily's head tightened in horror at the prospect, panic gripping her as she lay rigid in the chair as if she were at the dentist's—wondering for the millionth time how, or even if, she could ever break the news to Hunter.

'Have you been sunbathing?'

Swallowing down a rather too generous dose of headache tablets, Hunter squinted at Lily as she padded into the kitchen wrapped in a flimsy sarong and frantically trying to locate the very sheer, extortionately expensive silk stockings she'd purchased that afternoon.

'Just for a couple of hours.' Lily crossed her fingers behind her back as she simultaneously smiled and lied. She certainly wasn't going to tell Hunter that her healthy glow had been sprayed on!

It was hard to believe that something the size of a baked bean could wreak such havoc on her body, but even if she and Hunter had unequivocally proved that money didn't buy happiness, it certainly helped you to look good in your misery. Her hair, temporarily thick and glossy, and lashings of mascara and miracle eye drops had tired eyes falsely sparking—her skin, just as the brochure had *assured* her, beach-babe golden rather than keratin-tinged orange

'You look *very* nice.' Hunter actually managed a complement without adding a backhander!

'Have you seen my stockings?' Lily pulled back every cushion on the massive sofa. 'I know I bought them…'

'Sheer, black?'

'No, sheer, neutral.'

'Not guilty, then.' He attempted a smile at his rather pathetic joke but it faded midway, his fingers dashing to his temples, massaging them as he winced in sudden pain.

'Are you OK?' Lily paused in mid cushion hurl, actually looking at him for the first time since he'd come home and realising the stupidity of her question. He looked dreadful—his face as waxy and as pale as the huge lilies arranged in the entrance hall, smudges under his eyes so purple it looked like make-up. 'Hunter, maybe we should give tonight a miss.'

'I don't think so.' He grimaced, downing a

glass of water and promptly refilling it. 'People are paying a thousand dollars a ticket to see the happy couple.' He didn't finish his sentence, just tipped his water down the sink, stalked into the bedroom and promptly peeled off his clothes. 'Headache or not, I'm expected to turn up smiling—with you on my arm,' he added, naked, miserable and still impossibly sexy. 'You're the draw card.'

'Why?'

'Because you landed me!' He managed a flicker of smile. 'In case you forgot, I'm actually considered quite a catch.'

'Perhaps,' Lily answered as Hunter stalked off towards the shower. 'But, then, journalists don't have the pleasure of actually living with you twenty-four seven!'

Slipping on her dress, Lily struggled with the concealed zip at the back and then tied on her lethally high strappy sandals, before staring at her reflection in the full-length mirror. Strange that when everything was crumbling away she'd never looked better. Her dress was chocolate brown, elegant and simple, tapered at the waist, her expanding bust for once buxom, the spray-on tan, the glossy curls all giving the impression of glowing vitality and newly wedded bliss.

Hopefully the cameras, on this occasion, would lie!

'Thanks!' Devastatingly handsome in a tuxedo, Hunter stared ahead as the lift descended. 'For coming tonight.'

'It doesn't mean anything,' Lily attempted. Just because she was there it didn't mean she was staying, but Hunter misunderstood, his answer just confusing her further.

'It does to me.'

He actually held her hand as they entered the ball and she actually let him.

United in misery perhaps, but still united— and as they took their seats Lily was stunned at what he'd achieved, understood then the hours of work that must surely have gone into this night and why Hunter couldn't ever have called it off. Anyone who was *anyone* was there. Hunter had pulled an impressive A List out of the bag, who were sure to delve very deeply into their bottomless pockets. Lily blinked as she read the raffle prizes on offer and the price of each ticket!

Cruises and cars aplenty, even the privilege of Hunter Myles working personally on your portfolio just one of the goodies on offer.

'I'll buy the whole book, thanks!' Lily let out a shocked laugh. 'Are people actually buying these tickets?'

'Let's hope so.'

'Hunter!' Abigail's perfume was as heavy as her make-up, and Lily felt her stomach tighten as her nemesis placed a possessive hand on Hunter's shoulder and whispered in his ear. 'Sorry to drag him away from you.' Abigail added as Hunter stood up. 'But that's what happens, I'm afraid, when you're sitting next to the host.'

'I shouldn't be long. I just need to—'

'It's fine,' Lily interrupted, bracing herself for an evening spent on the outside of Emma and Jim's love bubble, without even the solace of a single glass of wine. But Emma remembered her manners, disengaging herself from Jim's loving gaze momentarily and turning to Lily.

'You…' she beamed '…are the very first to know!' Thrusting her hand under Lily's nose, Lily wasn't sure which was brighter—the gorgeous diamond or Emma's smile. 'He asked me this evening! Oh, Lily, I can't believe it.'

'Congratulations!' It sounded so paltry, but it was so, *so* heartfelt. Lily's eyes filled up with tears as she stared at the happy couple.

Love really did exist—because here it was for everyone to see.

Despite her doubts, despite her utter refusal to believe in it, somehow, looking at Emma, looking at her cousin Jim, proud and shy beside her, Lily knew she'd been very wrong.

Real love did exist—real love really could last a lifetime.

If it was bridged from both sides.

She loved Hunter.

There and then Lily admitted what she'd long known.

From the second he'd swept into her life she'd loved him, only he'd made it clear from the start that it could never happen and she'd been stupid enough to think she could play along. She'd clicked *I accept* on the hypothetical twelve-month contract without ever considering the small print—she was the one who had broken the rules.

'Sorry to keep disappearing!' He didn't sound remotely so, his distraction evident as he smoothed the evening along, working the tables, delivering a rousing speech with such impeccable wit and timing that even Lily was left reeling, wondering how on earth he managed it all. But when the tables had been cleared, when a very perfunctory dance had been all she'd been awarded by the master, when the other couples at the table were up dancing and even Emma and Jim were running out of polite conversation, Lily's patience started to run out.

Just where the hell was he?

Staring beyond Emma, her eyes working the

room to find him, with a jolt she saw *them* by the door. She watched as Hunter lowered his head to talk to Abigail, saw her red talons wrap around his arm as she gave him a tender squeeze, her beautiful, cunning face smiling tenderly at him. Lily felt the knife inside her twist further as, in an intimate gesture, Abigail stroked his hair back from his forehead, touched him in a way surely only a lover would.

The last flicker of false hope was doused for ever as he wrapped his arms around her and they wandered, entwined, out of the ballroom.

As he utterly humiliated her.

And all Lily knew was that she couldn't go on like this—couldn't sit in a ballroom, even if it was for charity, just to keep up appearances. Knew that with every day that passed her normality faded, that with every kiss, with every night spent in his arms it became easier to forgive the unthinkable, easier to accept that little piece of him he offered than to be left with nothing at all.

'Excuse me!' Picking up her bag, Lily tried to

disappear without making a scene, tried to pretend she was just nipping out to the loo, but Emma's eyes were frowning.

'Is everything OK, Lily?' she checked. 'Wait a second and I'll come with you.'

Which put paid to her rapid exit.

'I know he's practically ignored you all night.' Emma chewed her lip nervously as Lily blew her nose into a handkerchief, hateful tears escaping the second they hit the ladies'. 'But that's the way he is when he's working—and tonight *is* work, Lily. I haven't even told him about Jim and I. Once this ball's over things will calm down. He should never have taken it on.'

'It isn't that…' Lily snapped her lips together, Emma absolutely the last person she could reveal her plight to, but it scared her how much she wanted to. 'I'm just being silly…' Lily attempted a smile, but it was a rather poor effort.

'Come out and have some champagne.'

'I'll just stay here for a bit.' Lily shook her head. 'Try and make myself presentable.'

'Alone?' Emma checked, and Lily nodded, tears welling again in her eyes as Emma turned her wheelchair and left, smiling at her proud independence as she negotiated the doors. Knowing their friendship was probably at an end and missing her already.

It *was* all over.

Bypassing the raucous queue for a taxi, Lily chose to walk. Her high heels clipped as she walked along the river, oblivious to the occasional wolf whistle, too blinded with grief to care whether walking alone at this late hour was a wise move. She arrived at Hunter's apartment block and realised it never had been, nor would it ever be, home.

She'd tell him about the baby when she was ready, Lily decided, pressing the lift button and stepping inside. His reaction didn't worry her now. It was the baby that was her sole concern—and either way, whatever way he played it, she'd stay strong. For now she'd get her things and leave him a note, tell him she'd be in touch in a few days…

It never once entered her head that he'd have beaten her home.

Even when he was being his vilest, she'd never thought he'd stoop as blatantly low as this, but stepping out of the bedroom, smiling with malice, was Abigail.

'What are you doing here?'

'Actually, I could ask the same of you.' Abigail gave a small scoff of laughter. 'You just keep coming back for more, don't you?'

'Get out!' Lily spat the words like a hissing kitten as she flung open the front door. Abigail must have realised she was serious because after only a second of hesitation she picked up her bag and smartly walked out of the door.

'Oh, and, Lily!' Turning as she came to the lift, Lily saw the twist of a smile on Abigail's face as she called out to her. 'Happy birthday!'

He'd cheapened her more than she'd ever thought possible.

Stepping into the master bedroom, hearing the

soft, ever-present music, seeing his magnificent profile sprawled sideways, the white moonlight draining all the colour and leaving only grey.

The saddest colour, she thought as she tiptoed across the bedroom floor, it took away the blood red of his lips, the sparkle of his eyes, the swarthy colour of his complexion, yet it allowed for so much else.

Allowed her to see the duplicity of their union, the beauty that had blinded her to the impossibility of it all, the delusion she, like so many others clung to—that love might somehow make it work.

She stood for a minute, maybe two, watching the rise and fall of his chest as he slept, taking those precious seconds to capture his image for the final time, to take in his beauty while she still could. She didn't want to wake him up, didn't want his eyes to open, because when they did, truth would invade—a truth she couldn't live with—so she took that precious moment before it ended, held onto it just as long as she possibly could.

'I'm leaving.'

Two words that should have been shouted were instead softly spoken, yet the impact was just as deep. She watched as his body unfurled beneath the sheets, as crystal eyes clouded on opening.

'It's not what it looks like—'

'It doesn't matter anyway.' For the longest time he stared at her, waited for her to elaborate, and finally she did. 'It doesn't matter what happened tonight because I'm leaving anyway. I'm just not happy with you, Hunter.'

Any protest he was mustering faded then. Whatever it was on the tip of his tongue remained forever unsaid as he paid her the greatest of insults. He just let out a long weary sigh, turned on his side and, pulled the sheet up over his shoulders.

'Well, that's it, then.'

His boredom, his blatant dismissal of her was the final straw. She felt as if a fist had been rammed into her stomach, the pain so violent she thought she might vomit. His outline beneath the sheet was utterly still and suddenly

Lily felt like kicking him, felt like slapping him for his inaction,

'That's it?' Her voice was rising with every word, her whole body rigid with tension, every fibre in her being taut, her mounting fury fuelled by his inaction. That he could just lie there and take it as he reduced her to what she'd dreaded becoming—another woman whose heart he'd broken, another tearful female sobbing at the bitter end. 'I tell you I'm leaving and you just roll over and go to sleep!'

'Lily…' He pulled himself up on his elbow, opened his mouth to speak, but she beat him to it, the anger that had been curiously absent trickling in as she took in his naked form beneath the sheets, his rumpled clothes on the floor and the pungent smell of Abigail's perfume hanging in the air. 'It's not how it seems…'

'Don't!' She spat out the word. 'Don't even try, Hunter.' She'd never felt anger before—she'd *thought* she'd felt it. Sitting, reading her father's lover's letters had been a pretty good dress rehearsal, finding her fiancé in bed with her best friend an impressive warm-up, but it didn't compare to the churning rage sweeping through her now. Not churning, *boiling,* fury unleashing so rapidly it hurt, hurt so badly she wanted to inflict it, too, wanted to kick him out of his inactions, wanted him to feel a fraction of the agony that drenched her now.

'You really think you're better than everyone else—you really think that your money and looks somehow mean that you can write your own rules. Well, guess what?' She was shouting, really shouting, her anger rising as still he lay there, his eyes closed as if waiting for it pass, clearly more than used to emotional ends! 'I'm better than you! I'm better than the sham you offered, the tiny piece you were willing to provide of yourself! Whatever it is you're running from, I hope you never get there. Whatever you're drowning your emotions in, I hope it chokes you.'

There was a whole jewellery box there for the taking, a purse full of credit cards and a story that if sold could see her through to her pension, but Lily packed the bare minimum.

The very bare minimum.

Pulling off her rings, she laid them neatly on the bedside table, watched the lack of reaction from the man she loved, and almost in defiance picked up the remote and flicked off the stereo.

Turned off the noise that constantly clouded the issue.

'Give me that.' It was the most animated she'd seen him, his hand reaching out for the remote, grabbing at her wrist, but she shook him off, pulling out the batteries on the tiny piece of silver metal and hurling them across the room. 'Focus on what you've lost, Hunter. Stop drowning it out with emails or music or sex or whatever the latest fix is. Focus on what's walking out the door—and I'm telling you now that it's the best bloody thing that ever happened to you! I loved you, I know you don't want to hear it, I know you'll despise me for it—but I happened to love you.'

The lift took for ever to come, which out of

it all was the hardest part—standing in the foyer, tears choking her, having laid her heart on the line, waiting for the silver doors to take her away from it all.

Knowing had even if he had loved her even a little bit—he'd had plenty of time to follow her.

CHAPTER SIXTEEN

SINCE she'd found her father's letters, home hadn't really felt like it, yet strangely that was where Lily found solace.

Cocooned almost in a time when everything was right—when, no matter the problem, no matter how dire the circumstance or how extenuating the circumstances, it could somehow be made right.

And even if this was too big to fix, even if the problems that daunted her couldn't be soothed with a kiss and a smile, it was nice to retreat awhile, nice to lie on the quilt that had seen her through adolescence, to listen to the coming and goings of the family home and pause to regroup.

To hear the footsteps of her mother on the

stairs, the creak of the door and the welcome scent of coffee, toast, and if not understanding, just the sharing of unconditional love as her mum sat on the side of the bed and wrapped Lily in her arms to shield her from the appalling sadness. Because again it was clear there was no news for her mother to tell,

Hunter still hadn't rung.

'Couples have rows,' Catherine offered, for the hundredth time. 'You know I love you, but you have to talk to him. You can't just hide here, you have to face your problems as a couple, deal with them.'

'He doesn't love me.' There, she'd said it, admitted as much to her mother as she could without revealing all the sordid details, but Catherine just shook her head.

'Rubbish! He adores you,' Catherine admonished, and Lily pulled her hands over her ears, couldn't take the well-intended comfort. 'I know he loves you.'

'Mum—'

'He does,' Catherine insisted. 'He loves you

just as your father loved me. Marriages take work, Lily.'

She couldn't bear it, could hardly bear to lie there and be delivered a lecture from the most unwitting of victims, to be told the rules of love from someone who clearly hadn't a clue. She pulled the sheet higher, nestled in the pillows and braced herself for a vague response, prepared her mind for a grateful smile to her mother for supposedly making it all better.

'You think I don't know what I'm talking about, don't you?'

'I think things were different between you and Dad,' Lily answered carefully. 'The problems Hunter and I face…'

'Are more complicated,' her mother offered. 'More painful, more difficult? Just because you're younger, it doesn't mean you feel things more.'

'I wasn't saying that,' Lily attempted, but her words faded as her mother broke in.

'Your father had an affair…'

It was as if the universe had tipped on its axis,

the whole world spinning as Lily digested what her mother had said. Surely the books should be spinning off the shelves, the pictures collapsing under the weight of revelation, but as she peered out from under the sheet the room was exactly as she had left it. The only difference Lily could see, was the very real understanding in her mother's supposedly oblivious eyes, a different perspective on years of torture.

'No.' Though she'd known it for years, Lily still attempted to deny it, to squeeze the cork back into the bottle. But the genie was out, filling the room with an honesty that seeped into Lily's marrow, that erased so much more than deceit—it showed her the woman her mother had always been.

Revealed the child *she* still was.

'I could have killed him when I found out.' Catherine smiled down at her child, pushed back a strand of hair in a long-forgotten gesture. 'I was going to leave.'

'Why didn't you?'

'I actually did leave him—remember the time

we went to stay at Granny Meldrum's?' She gave a wistful smile and suddenly looked a decade younger than her years, and in that moment Lily was assailed with memories. Not the tired woman she saw now. Instead, she remembered her mother in a boxy suit, pursing her lips in the mirror of her grandmother's home before heading off to work, defiant, sexy and somehow proud.

'Are you saying that the two of you had broken up?' Lily shook her head. 'I don't remember any rows, I don't—'

'We kept it from you.' Catherine smiled. 'In fact, for the first couple of days I didn't even tell my mother why we were there, though she soon worked it out.'

'She knew?' Lily blinked. 'Granny Meldrum knew about Dad's affair? What on earth did she say?'

'Not what I wanted her to,' Catherine said. 'She pointed out that I'd changed—that since I'd gone back to work…' Catherine let out a long sigh and suddenly it wasn't her mother sitting on the bed but another woman, an older, wiser woman who maybe really did understand. 'There was a guy in the office, we flirted a bit and I suppose it all went to my head. Suddenly I wasn't just a wife and a mum, I was earning my own money, going out for drinks after work...' She shook her head and Lily was glad, because she didn't know if she'd ever have been able to ask her mother that question. 'I didn't have an affair, Lily, but I thought about it—and maybe in time, if I hadn't found out about your father, it would have happened.

'We worked it out, Lily. Both of us came to our senses and realised our mistakes, worked out together that we really did love each other.'

'You forgave him?'

'And he forgave me,' Catherine said softly. 'We had a rough patch, and, yes, it was hell at that time, but we were so, so much more than that, Lily. He was a wonderful husband, a great father...' Lily could almost *feel* Hunter in the room, *feel* his arms around her, understood now that it wasn't, nor ever had been her secret to keep or reveal or even attempt to understand. 'Look,' Catherine continued only this time Lily listened. 'I don't know what's gone on…' As the phone rang and Catherine went to answer it, Lily lay there, wishing it could be so, wishing that she and Hunter had some of the foundations of her parents' marriage to build on in desperate times.

'Lily.' Catherine's tentative voice broke into her thoughts and Lily's heart soared with hope, only to be dashed as she heard her mother's worried voice. 'That was a reporter from one of the news channels.'

'Just say I'm not here,' Lily answered quickly. 'Tell them you don't know anything about the break-up.' Frowning, she watched as her mother, instead of heading back out to the hall, came and sat down on the bed, her eyes widening as she took in her mother's pale face, felt her mother's hands wrap around hers, just as she had when she'd come into the room one morning and told her that her father had died.

'They want to know if I've heard anything from you at the hospital.'

'The hospital?' She didn't understand, could hear her voice coming from a long way off as her mind darted to Hunter, as tiny shards of rec-ollection pieced together.

'He was found collapsed this morning, that's all I know.'

CHAPTER SEVENTEEN

'How could you?' Emma's accusing face wasn't the greeting Lily had been expecting as she was led into the emergency unit's interview room. She'd expected a roomful of people, but instead it was Jim and Emma, huddled together and waiting for news as Lily breathlessly joined them 'How could you have left him?'

'Not now, Em.' Jim wrapped an arm around Emma and gave his cousin a wan smile. 'I'm sure she had her reasons.'

'I didn't know he was sick.' Trembling, shaking, Lily sank into one of the chairs, watched her knees bob up and down as Emma gave an incredulous snort.

'Abigail said that by the time she left him last night he was practically unconscious, that the only reason she left him was because you'd come home.'

'That isn't what happened.' Lily's teeth were chattering. She'd deal with Abigail later, deal with her in the fullness of time, but right now all she wanted to know about was Hunter, to find out what the hell had happened. 'Where's Hunter? How is he?'

'What do you care?' Emma sneered, and for the first time Lily realised with horror that somehow she knew. 'I spoke to Hunter in briefly in Emergency—he told me the truth, so you can cut out the crocodile tears, you can stop pretending you care how he is. Oh, but, then again, you've got a huge vested interest in Hunter's health—what a merry widow you'll be!'

'What's wrong with him?' Lily demanded, fear, absolute fear gripping her, and guilt, too, at her unwitting part in this, that she'd stood screaming like a banshee while he'd lain there ill.

'They're not sure. He's having a brain scan. They've called in the best neurologist, so hopefully we'll have some answers soon.'

Thankfully Jim broke the appalling stone wall she'd been thrown behind. 'He's been ill for a few weeks now, according to Abigail. He went to see a doctor yesterday after he came back from Singapore. He was booked in to have some tests on Monday.'

'Oh, God.' Lily buried her face in her hands, could actually picture his tired, grey face so clearly it was if he were right there in front of her. She wanted to reach out to him as she hadn't back then, to take him by the hand and lead him to bed, replaying so many, many things in her mind now—the fistfuls of painkillers, the unsteady gait, the vile black temper, all that time he'd been ill! 'Oh, Hunter.' Tears were trickling through her fingers, thinking of him so tall and proud lying attached to some wretched machine so scared and ill. Whatever had gone on between them, whatever he felt about her, it couldn't extinguish the love that burnt there— for Lily at least.

'Oh, please.' The disgust in Emma's voice was blisteringly evident. 'Save the tears for the press. I trusted you, Lily. I sat there and poured my heart out to you and all the time you must have been laughing inside. All this time you were lying about wanting to be here!'

'Never! I genuinely cared for you, Emma.' Lily looked at her sister-in-law, and it was like looking in a mirror—the raw pain of confusion and humiliation there, as it had been for Lily when she'd found the letters—and she listened as Emma replayed their time together with the wretched twist of deception.

'You never cared. It was all a sham, your marriage, our friendship. I didn't want a false friend.' Emma was sobbing so hard she could barely get the words out. 'I just wanted my brother to be happy, to find some peace!'

'I want the same thing for him.' Lily's voice was so small it was barely there, the word whispered through pale lips. 'You don't understand—'

'I understand this much.' Emma stared at her coolly, her tears drying up, displaying some of the strength that had seen her through this most vile of years. 'You walked out on a very sick man who happens to be a very wealthy one. Right now your filthy secret won't leave this room, but I swear, if anything happens to my brother I'll fight you to the bitter end—you won't see a single cent!'

The horror of what she was accusing her of barely had time to register. The door opened and a red-eyed Abigail came in, followed by a doctor who introduced himself. They must have hauled him off the golf course because he was still wearing his spikes, and it was easier to focus on that than the horror of Emma's words, easier to focus on incidentals as she braced herself for news.

'We're just starting to get some test results in. It would seem there's an infection somewhere, but till we get the lumbar puncture and CT scan results back, I can't tell you much more. He's resting quietly in a private room at the moment.'

'I'll go and sit with him.' Emma's hands moved to the wheels as Abigail turned on her heel, clearly about to follow suit.

'Just one at a time,' the doctor said. 'He's

heavily sedated at the moment—right now, more than anything he needs now to rest.'

'*I'll* sit with him.' Lily almost didn't recognize her own voice, despite the blizzard of emotion in her brain, despite the tears rolling down her face, her voice, in contrast, was measured and controlled.

'Don't be ridiculous.' Emma didn't even deign to give her a glance as she wheeled her chair through the door, Abigail already marching on ahead towards the lifts. 'Why on earth would we let you near him?'

'Because he's my husband.' Wiping her face with back of her hand, Lily turned to the doctor. 'I believe, as his next of kin, I have every right to be with him.'

Every legal right apparently, but as she saw the look on Emma's face, as the doctor nodded and a nurse escorted her to the room where Hunter was being monitored, morally Lily wasn't so sure. What right did she have to make this or any decision for him? What right did she have to keep his sister from him, to keep the staff he'd hand-picked away, when perhaps he needed them most?

Tiptoeing into the room, she felt her heart spasm in wretched pain—tried to convince herself that he was just sleeping. Tried and failed, because sleep was restful, sleep relaxed and replenished, yet Hunter looked ravaged. Despite the sedation and the darkened room, his body twitched with tension, his face grey and lined, as if the world had moved forward a decade. Lily's guilt multiplied, as if somehow this was her fault, as if somehow she'd done this to him.

To them.

She held his hand and it felt so cold she held it with two hands, tried to infuse warmth into him, stared down at the long slender fingers just as she had on the night they'd met, saw the bitten nails of whatever doubts plagued him and willed him to relax, to let whatever it was that was feeding from the drip into his body do its work, to take away his wretchedness, even for a little while.

'I'm sorry.' Her voice was thick with tears and even if he couldn't hear her she said it anyway. 'Sorry for not seeing you weren't well, sorry for messing up…' A sob shuddered on her lips and her nose ran. She even managed a strangled laugh, glimpsed the appalled expression that would surely be on Hunter's face if only he could see her now. 'Sorry for loving you.'

A hand was on her shoulder and, startled, Lily jumped, turning around to see Emma, who had silently entered the room.

'I'm sorry, too.' Eyes as blue as Hunter's stared back at her. 'You really do love him, don't you?'

'Not that he'd be pleased to hear it,' Lily sniffed. 'That wasn't part of the deal.'

'What I said back there.' Emma gave a helpless shake of her head. 'I just couldn't believe I'd got things so wrong. I was just so embarrassed, so appalled that you'd married to appease me…'

'It wasn't like that,' Lily said, her mind racing to come up with some magical answer, to take the sting out of Emma's wound. But nothing she said now could obliterate the past—only the truth might provide a balm. 'At least, it wasn't for me.'

'I know.' Emma stared at her brother for an age but then the tears started again, real tears that came from deep inside that needed to be addressed. And as much as it hurt to let go of Hunter's hand, Lily did so, knew from the little she did know about him that it was what Hunter would want. She followed Emma outside into the stark white hall to hear and reveal the stark black truth.

'I thought he was sleeping with Abigail,' Lily admitted. 'Last night I saw him with his arms around her—that's the real reason I was crying at the ball.'

'But he nearly passed out at the ball,' Emma explained. 'That's why Abigail brought him home. He didn't tell you he was leaving because he physically couldn't—all he wanted apparently was to get the hell out of there without making a fuss.'

'I can see that now,' Lily admitted. 'But when I got home…' She closed her eyes at the horrible image, could still see Abigail's smirk as she'd come out of the bedroom, still didn't really know if she was just fooling herself. 'Abigail let me think they'd been together. Maybe they weren't last night, but I still don't know if he's been unfaithful.'

'What if he has?' Emma voiced the difficult question. 'What if he made a mistake?'

'Then it's over.' Lily gave a tight nod, balled her fists and held onto conviction. 'It has to be. I told him when I agreed to the marriage that it was the one thing I'd never forgive.'

'Why does he have to sabotage everything?' Emma said. 'I've tried to help him. I've pleaded with him to slow down—when I heard about your group I thought that maybe if he went…'

Suddenly Lily was still. For the second time in a single day her past, her conviction utterly, utterly distorted, the sure ground she'd stood on shifting further.

'He came to New Beginnings to check it out

for you,' Lily whispered, remembering again his arrogant face on entering the club, his palpable boredom at the proceedings and his absolute lack of desire to be there.

'*Supposedly* for me,' Emma corrected. 'I wasn't the one that needed help. I'd already made my peace—I was more than ready to move on with my life. It was Hunter that was struggling. Look, I'm not saying it's been easy for me, but for all my injuries, for all I'm stuck in this chair, it doesn't come close to what Hunter's suffering.'

'I don't understand.' Only *now* she could admit it, only *now* could she confess her terrifying helplessness to reach him, only *now* reveal to Emma just how little she knew. 'Just what happened in Singapore? He told me he wasn't driving, that he wasn't even in the car—'

'He arranged the whole night,' Emma broke in, and Lily closed her eyes in regret for him. 'He was in Singapore on business while I was playing there, and he got it into his head that if our parents only heard me play, if we were just together for one night, if we got Mum and Dad out of the house and enjoyed each other's company, maybe things would be different. They didn't want to come, but Hunter sort of railroaded them into it. Organised the flight, the hotel, even sent a car to their house to pick them up.'

'Oh, God!'

'They saw me play and then he got called away. We were at this bar and Hunter had something urgent to attend to, so he said he'd meet us back at the hotel for dinner. The accident happened then.

'Do you see now why he blames himself?' Emma's face was chalk white. 'He blames himself and, much as I tell him not to, the truth is I fully understand why, because in my darkest moments sometimes I've blamed him, too. If he'd just left things alone, hadn't inter-fered, then Mum and Dad would still be here, I'd still be walking…' Emma snapped her mouth closed, startled eyes darting to Lily's as if she should somehow be flinching, should somehow berate or reprimand her. But Lily gave the gentlest smile of understanding.

'It's OK,' Lily said softly, kneeling down and wrapping her arms around Emma's. 'It's OK to feel like that at times.'

'Is it?' Emma gulped.

'You wouldn't be human if you didn't,' Lily ventured. 'Maybe it's what Hunter needs to hear. As much as the truth hurts, sometimes it's needed.'

'Stupid thing is, it turns out that he *was* right.' Emma pulled away, glimpsed a world that was still standing after her revelation. 'Mum and Dad were the happiest I've ever seen them that night in the bar before the accident. They told me that that night had been the best of their lives, that they were proud of us both...'

Perhaps they had, perhaps they hadn't. Lily truly didn't know if Emma was using poetic licence to distort the painful memory, or if indeed she was telling the truth. All Lily knew was that if it made the agony more bearable then it was something Emma needed to believe...

Hunter, too.

* * *

'Mrs Myles?' The doctor had changed out of his golf spikes into smart leather shoes, and she jumped at the title. 'I've just got your husband's results in.'

And she could have faced it alone, could have sent Emma away, but today had nothing to do with who deserved to hear what—or who was right and who was wrong. Today was about Hunter and, holding Emma's hand, the two women braced themselves to hear the news.

How long she sat there staring, Lily didn't know. Time had no meaning as again she watched the rise and fall of his chest. Once he opened those eyes, squinted at her in the way that always melted her heart.

'Sleep,' Lily said softly.

'You're here?' She sensed his confusion, moved quickly to douse it—touched his beautiful face with her hand and willed him to rest, knowing instinctively now the right words to say to him.

'I'm here because I want to be.'

She watched the moon move across the sky,

watched the sun rise on another morning, watched bag upon bag of fluids seep into his veins until the sun rose on yet another day, stripping the grey and tipping the world into colour, a lazy blush crawling into the room, his cyanosed lips flushing red, the exhausted rise and fall of his chest slipping into an easier rhythm. And for the first time in her adult life Lily allowed herself to be looked after. Sipped the coffee Emma brought, squeezed her hand as she disappeared as silently as she'd come—felt from her sister-in-law the acknowledgment of the love she had for her brother, real love, because whether or not he felt the same was immaterial. Even if she had to leave him because of what he'd done, she'd never stop loving him. True love didn't have to be reciprocated to exist.

'Hey.' Hunter blanched at the sunlight that bathed him, winced as the pain caught up with him. 'I thought that you'd left me.'

'Believe me, I tried.'

'I'm sorry.' He stared right at her as he said

it. 'Sorry for putting you through this. I never wanted you to find out.'

'Well, I did,' she said simply. Now was not the time for venom, now not the time to impale him with her pain 'And I'm not here to make things harder for you now. I'm actually here to say sorry, too—sorry for not realising you were sick when I shouted at you.'

'I wanted you to leave me.' His brutal admission inflicted a pain that was physical and Lily's vow to stay calm, to not cry at this part, crumbled, along with her pride.

'You could have just told me that.' Lily blew her fringe skywards, tried to keep her voice calm. 'You didn't have to sleep with Abigail to make me leave.'

'I never slept with Abigail.'

She wanted almost to doubt him because it scared her how badly she wanted to believe him, yet truly she did. Now was not the time for lies. His voice was so unwavering, his eyes so direct she knew she was hearing the truth.

'If I told you I was sick you'd have stayed, but

for all the wrong reasons.' Again he confused her, again she lost the thread of the conversation. Massaging her temples, she dragged in a breath, tried to fathom what on earth he was talking about. 'You'd have stayed out of duty.'

'What duty?' Lily frowned. 'Hunter…' His words were starting to sink in—like the letters in a game of Scrabble, a seemingly jumbled mess but which, arranged properly, started to make sense. But she needed clarification, needed that one missing part before she made her next move. 'Hunter, what do you think is wrong with you?' He didn't answer, just stared up at the ceiling as she gently explained what the doctors had told her. 'You've got a bacterial infection,' Lily explained softly, 'a serious form of labrynthitis.'

'You're telling me I've got an ear infection?' A laugh shot out of his lips, but it changed midway, and Lily glimpsed the burden he'd been carrying.

'Hey,' Lily said gently, reaching out and taking his hand, feeling the tight grip of his fingers as he held on, as he struggled to stay afloat. She held on, held on to him for just a little bit longer before she regretfully let go, before he took her under, too. 'You're not the only one to let your imagination run wild—I had you pegged as an alcoholic or drug addict.' She tried to keep her voice light, only she wasn't smiling. Tears spilled down her cheeks as she stared down at him. 'What did you think was wrong with you?'

'The same as my father…' Cold with shock, she glimpsed his fear then, his very real, very genuine fear—the burden he had been carrying since the moment they had met. 'I thought I was going to end up doing to you what he did to her. I kept getting dizzy…'

'The infection caused the unsteadiness and the headaches,' Lily explained, 'but it's not just that. The doctor said you're exhausted, Hunter. You're not just tired or a bit run down, you're completely and utterly exhausted. The doctor said he had no idea how you managed to fly in your condition, that it would have been agony.

Why didn't you say something? Why didn't you just tell me?'

'Because it's not your job to worry.'

He said it again, only this time, instead of running off, she faced him, answered him with his own words. 'It's not that easy, though, is it?'

'You'd have stayed, wouldn't you?' He fixed her with the bluest eyes she'd ever seen or would see, his powerful question the most intense she'd ever confronted.

'Not for the reasons you're thinking.'

'I'm not talking about money, Lily.' He wasn't—that much at least he didn't have to tell her. Even if it had been a marriage of convenience, money had long since ceased to be the issue. 'You'd have stayed because you felt you had to, out of duty, because, morally or legally, you considered yourself my wife.'

'No.' She shook her head, closed her eyes on his piercing glare, terrified of revealing the true depth of her feelings, scared of revealing the truth.

'Lily.' His hand released hers, cupping her

face now, daring her to look at him, but still she refused. 'I'd rather have died alone than have someone looking after me out of duty.'

'Promise?' She shuddered the question out, forced her eyes open to take in his confused reaction. 'Promise me that you'll remember that feeling, promise me that you'll be honest with me now.'

Confused, he nodded

'I'm pregnant.' Hunter's face was absolutely still. Not by a flicker did he divulge his reaction. 'And, like you, I'd rather be alone than have you stay out of duty—I couldn't stand it.'

'You wouldn't have to.' He took her hand, sat up a bit in the bed, and even if he was sick, he was still the strong one. 'Lily, a baby isn't going to make us work, a baby isn't enough reason to be together.'

'I know,' she gulped, hating the truth but grateful for his honesty.

'Unless that's what we both want.' She felt her heart stop in her chest, honesty a breath away, and she was scared to take it, so Hunter did it for them. 'Unless we both actually want to be together.'

It was the worst moment to think of her appearance, but good old vanity attempted to prevail, reminding her of her puffy eyes and running nose, reminding her that even on a hospital bed with a thousand tubes attached she was still facing the most beautiful man she had ever seen and showing him the most fragile, vulnerable part of her heart.

'You don't believe in love,' Lily pointed out.

'Neither do you.' Hunter smiled. 'Philistine.'

'And you're way too controlling.' Lily clutched at straws as he dragged her back in. 'I don't know if I want to spend my life—'

'I was scared of losing you.' His simple admission stopped her in her tracks, his honesty the revelation she needed. 'I was scared of you balancing on a chair at that bloody house, scared of you driving around, scared of *anything* that might take you away from me. I know I was very wrong. I just didn't want anything to happen to you.'

'The way it did to them?' Lily offered, because she knew what he must have been feeling, just had never considered it might have been related to her.

'I've lost or damaged everyone I've ever loved and I couldn't bear to it to happen to you. Couldn't bear the thought of you getting hurt. Couldn't bear the thought of you leaving, but at the same time I couldn't cope with the thought of you staying, only to end up looking after me.

'I love you.' Hunter said it very slowly and very clearly so there was absolutely no room for doubt. 'I love you because you're funny and kind and good. I love you because, whether or not you love me, you'd have looked after me even though that truly terrified me. I love you because for the first time in my life I actually wanted to come home…' He was staring right at her as he spoke. 'For the first time in my life I actually felt as if I *had* a home.'

'You really love me?' she checked, and he laughed.

'I love you because even when I'm saying it

over and over, you still don't believe it. God, Lily.' Exasperation crept into his voice. 'I'm lying here telling you all this like some blubbering idiot and I don't even know how you feel. Isn't that proof enough?'

'You know how I feel,' Lily shot back. 'Why else would I have put up with you?'

'Oh, I can think of a few reasons—because I'm loaded, because I'm brilliant in bed, because you're pregnant and feel that you have no choice…' He was joking, sort of, but he was also letting her in, allowing her to glimpse his fears. Both of them were being honest for the very first time, and it felt wonderful.

'They're not reasons to stay, Hunter, they're excuses.' Lily smiled, treated him to a short, sharp lecture just as she had the night they'd met.

And he confronted her, just as he had the night they'd met.

'Stop evading the issue.'

'I'm not.'

'So what's the real reason you'd be staying?'

She took a deep breath, held it for a moment

before diving into the giddy world of being Hunter Myles' s *real* wife, before saying the words she truly thought she never would.

'I'm staying because I love you.'

EPILOGUE

'I THINK Cory's getting a tooth!'

Emma's voice carried from the lounge to the kitchen where both Hunter and Lily were frantically trying to prepare a gourmet meal in a matter of minutes while Emma nursed her nephew. Somehow they had to cover up the fact that they'd forgotten that they had asked Jim and Emma to come over for dinner tonight.

Chaos was the norm these days—delightfully so. This was home now. No catered dinners. No working to the housekeeper's schedule. It was chaotic bliss.

Hunter, thanks to finally mastering the art of delegation, was home far more often, only Lily was working now. Her studies were complete, she had a small but steady stream of patients. Just another busy couple juggling the demands of one small baby and two careers—and it was wonderful.

'Is he sleeping through the night yet?' Emma called.

'Is she referring to you or the baby?' Lily grinned before cheekily calling back the answer to both questions. 'If I'm lucky I manage four, maybe five hours!

'Open this,' she added, handing a jar of sauce to Hunter, who was pretending to be offended. 'There's some garlic bread in the freezer.'

'I hope you haven't gone to too much trouble…' Both women's voices trailed off as Emma wheeled into the kitchen and surveyed the chaos, clearly realising they hadn't gone to *any* trouble at all.

'Em, we forgot.' Hunter actually winced. 'Sorry! You know, new baby and everything…'

'That's OK.' Emma attempted a martyred expression but it dissolved into a burst of giggles. 'Actually, we both forgot, too. We only remembered we were supposed to be coming over for dinner half an hour ago!'

'Why don't we ring for Chinese?' Hunter suggested, but Emma wrinkled up her nose. 'Or Indian.'

'Pasta would be great,' Emma broke in. 'Actually, I'm a bit off my food—were you like that, Lily?' Emma's cheeks were flaming. 'When you were pregnant?'

'God, no.' Hunter answered for her. 'She ate like a…' He didn't finish, realisation hitting at the same time Jim joined Emma at the kitchen door and handed him his son. 'You mean…'

'That's what we've been trying to tell you since we got here, but you were too busy rushing around, fixing dinner. We're having a baby!' Emma's face was shining. 'It was confirmed this afternoon. I've had a scan and everything and it turns out that I'm ten weeks pregnant!'

'And you'll be OK?' Hunter checked. 'I mean, with…' He took a breath then forced the words out. 'What with your injuries and everything?'

'I'll need a Caesarean section,' Emma explained softly, 'and I might not quite make it to term, but apart from that the doctor's pretty confident it will be a normal pregnancy.'

He hugged her, held little Cory in between them and hugged his sister. And Lily knew how big this was for him, knew because he'd told her that he was scared it might never happen for her—knew that with this wonderful news they were moving ever further on. And when Emma and Jim drifted out to the lounge, Hunter confirmed what she was thinking, stared down at his son for the longest time before looking over at Lily.

'I wanted this for her.' Hunter attempted to voice what he was thinking. 'When we had Cory...' His voice thickened with emotion. 'I just wanted her to know some of the joy.' And this time Lily didn't drag it out of him, just helped him along, guilt a visitor rather than a companion in his life now.

'She's doing great, Hunter. Both of you are doing fine. Your parents would be really proud.'

'Do you reckon?' Normally he'd have waved her words away—his parents and their appalling relationship, still a minefield where they rarely ventured—but, staring down at Corey, it was Hunter prolonging the conversation. 'I really don't know how they'd feel if they were alive, but this much I do know...' Blue eyes looked up from his son to her, the three of them locked in an endless circle of love. 'I'm proud. Proud of you, proud of me...proud of us.'

MILLS & BOON PUBLISH EIGHT LARGE PRINT TITLES A MONTH. THESE ARE THE EIGHT TITLES FOR NOVEMBER 2007.

BOUGHT: THE GREEK'S BRIDE
Lucy Monroe

THE SPANIARD'S BLACKMAILED BRIDE
Trish Morey

CLAIMING HIS PREGNANT WIFE
Kim Lawrence

CONTRACTED: A WIFE FOR THE BEDROOM
Carol Marinelli

THE FORBIDDEN BROTHER
Barbara McMahon

THE LAZARIDIS MARRIAGE
Rebecca Winters

BRIDE OF THE EMERALD ISLE
Trish Wylie

HER OUTBACK KNIGHT
Melissa James

Pure reading pleasure

MILLS & BOON PUBLISH EIGHT LARGE PRINT TITLES A MONTH. THESE ARE THE EIGHT TITLES FOR DECEMBER 2007.

TAKEN: THE SPANIARD'S VIRGIN
Lucy Monroe

THE PETRAKOS BRIDE
Lynne Graham

THE BRAZILIAN BOSS'S INNOCENT MISTRESS
Sarah Morgan

FOR THE SHEIKH'S PLEASURE
Annie West

THE ITALIAN'S WIFE BY SUNSET
Lucy Gordon

REUNITED: MARRIAGE IN A MILLION
Liz Fielding

HIS MIRACLE BRIDE
Marion Lennox

BREAK UP TO MAKE UP
Fiona Harper

MILLS & BOON
Pure reading pleasure

1107 Rom L